An American Family Chronicle

I0600236

GENERATIONS
of ENDURANCE

JAMES D. HAMILTON

Front cover image: Portrait of *Susannah Clarissa Iler Hamilton Heacock*, c. 1860s (family archival photograph; used with permission).

Back cover image: 1845 deed to the Defiance County courthouse property, signed by William C. Holgate (family archival photograph; used with permission).

Cover and interior formatting by KUHN Design Group | kuhndesigngroup.com

GENERATIONS OF ENDURANCE
An American Family Chronicle

Copyright © 2025 by James D. Hamilton
All rights reserved.

Published in the United States by **Hamilton Heritage Press**, a division of Ambulatory Medical Management, LLC, Spencerville, Indiana, USA

ISBNs:
Hardcover: 979-8-9941867-2-5
Paperback: 979-8-9941867-1-8
eBook: 979-8-9941867-0-1

Library of Congress Control Number: 2025926916

Printed in the United States of America

AUTHOR'S NOTE

This book is the product of years of research, family memory, and historical exploration. It draws from verified records, oral traditions, local histories, early regional documents, and the preserved recollections of relatives who carried these stories across generations.

Where the historical record is clear, the events and relationships are presented as faithfully as possible. Where the record is silent, incomplete, or lost—as is often the case in early American family histories—I have used historically grounded inference to fill the gaps. Some scenes, settings, and conversations are imagined, but they are built upon the known realities of the period, the geography, the culture, and the lives of the people whose footsteps shaped this story.

This work is not a genealogical proof study, nor is it intended to stand as a definitive historical biography of any one person. Rather, it is a narrative chronicle inspired by the enduring arc of three intertwined families—the Pennocks, the Hamiltons, and the Heacocks—whose paths carried them from England and Ireland, through the landscapes of Pennsylvania, and ultimately into the growing frontier town of Defiance, Ohio.

It is, at heart, a tribute: to endurance, to migration, to aspiration, and to the quiet strength of ordinary families who built a life out of the uncertain world they inherited.

To my Aunt, **Eleanor Hamilton,**
whose patience, curiosity, and unwavering devotion
to our family's past lit the first spark of this journey.

Long before the conveniences of digital archives, searchable databases, or online repositories, she practiced genealogy in its truest form—with notebooks worn at the edges, handwritten charts, and careful letters sent to county clerks, historical societies, distant relatives, and local librarians who guarded the old records. She sifted through courthouse basements, cemetery ledgers, and family Bibles, piecing together a legacy one fragile page at a time.

She preserved what might otherwise have been lost. And she handed that legacy to me.

This book is the continuation of the path she began, a journey now forty years in the making—one that has shaped me more than I ever expected.

And somewhere deep within that journey, I often find myself wishing for a conversation I will never have: A quiet moment on a porch beside **Susannah Clarissa Iler Hamilton/Heacock**, to hear her voice, her truths, her wisdom, and the stories only she could tell.

This work is, in a way, my attempt to listen.
—*Jim Hamilton*

CONTENTS

PREFACE

There are lives whose stories are written in ledgers and court papers, in old census lines, in brittle marriage records and worn burial stones. And then there are the stories carried in memory—the ones whispered on porches, tucked into family Bibles, or held gently in the pauses between generations. This book belongs to both.

The world that shaped the Pennock, Iler, Hamilton, and Heacock families was one of movement—across ocean waters, along rough wagon roads, through the deep forests and The Great Black Swamp mud of early Ohio. Their lives were bound first by the quiet meetinghouses of Chester County, Pennsylvania, then by the roar of General Anthony Wayne's soldiers at the confluence of the Maumee and the Grand Glaize, years later called the Auglaize River, followed by the rising hum of canal commerce and the shriek of iron rails carving their way into the West.

Much of what is known comes from documents: estate papers, Quaker minutes, census rolls, deeds, wills, city directories, hotel ledgers, and the occasional preserved letter. But woven between these facts are threads of memory, inference, and the lived texture of the world these families moved through. Some scenes in this book rise directly from the historical record; others are shaped from the logic of time and place, grounded in what is known but necessarily imaginative where the record falls silent. Every conjectural moment is rooted carefully in the environment these ancestors inhabited—in the customs, hardships, and possibilities that framed their lives.

The Poor School of Chester County, the Quaker silence of the Pennocks, the loss that shaped Jane (Pennock) Iler and her daughters, the quiet endurance that carried Susannah Clarissa across wilderness and grief—all of these are real. So are the hotels that bore the Heacock name, the mills that fed early Defiance, the canal locks that brought both travelers and opportunity, and the fierce resilience that families carried with them from the worn soil of Pennsylvania to the heavy timberlands of Northwest Ohio.

The story is enriched by the historical presence of the Wayne family—not as blood kin, but as an unexpected parallel line of influence. The Pennocks lived near the Waynes in Pennsylvania long before Defiance existed, never knowing that generations later their descendants would settle in the very town General Anthony Wayne founded. Such intersections remind us that history often turns on quiet proximities—families living side by side, unaware of how their separate paths will one day converge.

Yet this book is not only a chronicle of events. It is a story of endurance—of mothers who held families together when poverty and loss threatened to undo them; of husbands who sought their fortunes in new towns and on new rails; of children who grew up with the smell of woodsmoke and canal water in the air; of a community built not by chance, but by the determined hands of pioneers whose names still echo in the stones of Riverside Cemetery.

At its heart, it is the story of Susannah Clarissa—a woman who lived long enough to see the wilderness become a town, the town become a center of industry, and the center of industry become a home for generations still to come. From the porch of her daughter's house, she looked back over a life that stretched from hardship to opportunity to fulfillment, and in her reflection lies the thread that ties this entire history together.

The families who fill these pages were ordinary people by the measures of their own day. And yet the convergence of their journeys—Pennock, Iler, Hamilton, Heacock—helped build a place called Defiance, and in doing so left a legacy far greater than they ever knew.

This book is their story.

And it is, in many ways, the story of how a town—and a family—came to be.

CHAPTER ONE

THE WORLD THAT SPLIT BETWEEN JAMES AND WILLIAM

To understand the choice that stood before men like Christopher Pennock, you must first understand that the world in the 1680s was not governed by laws alone. It was governed by fear and memory.

England had already lived through a civil war once in living memory. Fathers had fought sons. Kings had lost their heads—quite literally. Churches had burned. Neighborhoods had been divided against themselves. People still remembered the sound of boots in the night, of soldiers taking grain, horses, men, even children.

So when James II came to the throne in 1685, it was not just another coronation. It was a tremor running through the soil.

James was Catholic in a country that had fought and bled to be Protestant. He did not simply worship differently; in the minds of many, he represented a return to foreign influence, authoritarian rule, and papal power. To thousands of Englishmen and most Irish Protestants, he was not just a king—he was a threat to their land, their religion, and their children's future.

And yet, to many Irish Catholics, James was hope.

For the Irish, he symbolized the possibility of restoration—of lands taken, rights stripped away, dignity long denied. To them, William of Orange was an invader, a foreign prince landing with an army, arriving not as a savior, but as another conqueror.

So the world divided not by politics alone, but by identity.

In taverns, in farmhouses, in Quaker gatherings, in Anglican churches, conversation turned toxic. Friend stopped speaking to friend. Brother eyed brother. Husbands and wives whispered in bed at night behind shuttered windows.

Everywhere there was the same question:

Which world will survive?

AND WHAT OF THE QUAKERS?

Quakers did not believe in kings by divine right. They did not believe in state churches. They believed the Light of God lived within every person.

This was seen as dangerous.

They did not swear oaths—which meant, in the eyes of the government, they could not be trusted in court.

They did not bear arms—which meant, in the eyes of the state, they were cowards or traitors.

They refused to bow, to kneel, to remove their hats, to speak in false deference.

And for that…

They were beaten. Imprisoned. Fined. Stripped of property.

Christopher Pennock's imprisonment was not an accident; it was policy.

The government feared anyone who did not outwardly pledge loyalty to the king and crown in the prescribed way. Silence was seen as rebellion. Neutrality looked like resistance. Peace was seen as disloyalty.

When Quakers met in quiet homes, when they sat in silence together, the authorities viewed it as a conspiracy. In the eyes of the state, if you did not kneel to the king, you meant to overthrow him.

So, Christopher was seized because the government believed that religious independence was the first step toward political rebellion.

In that world, even peace was treason.

THE PATH TO KILLHOUSE

By the time the bailiffs came through the rain-slick streets of Cork in 1660, Christopher Pennock already knew the sound of boots on stone.

The meetinghouse lay in a side lane near the river Lee, where the smell of tar and fish mixed with the sharp tang of wet wool. Inside, men and women sat in stillness, hats on their heads, listening for the Inward Light that George Fox had told them was nearer than their own breath. They had no altar, no priest, no chalice—just silence and the occasional tremor of a voice when someone felt moved to speak.

When the door banged open, the silence broke like thin glass.

"By order of the mayor," the bailiff called, his words echoing against bare plaster. "You are unlawfully assembled."

Christopher rose with the others. He was still a young man then, not yet the weathered shopkeeper and landholder he would become, but already marked: plain coat, no lace, no hat-doffing, a stubbornness in the set of his jaw. They took him and several others to prison for "meeting together for the exercise of that religion," as the record would later say. It would not be the last time.

Prison in 17th-century Cork was not a place of clean iron bars and orderly records. It was a low, damp room that stank of straw, sweat, and the sour tang of human waste. Rats moved in the dark; water seeped down stone walls. Quakers were kept with common criminals. They could be held for days or months, depending on the whim of magistrates or the persistence of local priests demanding tithes. And always there was the pressure of money: fines the family could not easily pay, goods seized in lieu of coin, stock taken from shop or pasture.

For Christopher, each imprisonment was a double blow: first to his body, then to his trade. When the church wardens seized "forty-nine yards of stuff" from his shop—a bolt of cloth worth several pounds—they were not just punishing a stubborn heretic. They were stripping the family's livelihood from the shelves, yard by yard.

Dorothy, his wife, tried to keep the business going while he sat in the dark.

She was a Harwood, steady and practical, with hands that were never still. The Cork meeting recorded the birth of their son John in the summer of 1665, then their daughter Hannah, then their little Sarah. In between births and funerals, she measured cloth, weighed buttons, and kept a wary eye on the door, never knowing when the priest's man or the church warden might appear.

When Dorothy sickened in 1671, the children crowded around her bed in the narrow house above the shop. The Friends came and sat in silence, broken only by prayer and the muffled noise of the street below. She died in the fifth month of that year, and the Cork meeting noted it in a few spare lines, as they did for so many others.

For Christopher, the house felt abruptly hollow. The bed was too wide. The shop too quiet. Grief pressed in where Dorothy's steady presence had been.

He might have remarried anyone: a widow from the meeting, a quiet woman from town. Instead, his life bent sharply toward the Colletts.

MARY OF KILLHOUSE

Mary Collett did not belong to the cramped streets of Cork. She belonged to Killhouse, a name that sounded harsher than the place looked.

Clonmel in Tipperary sat on the river Suir, its surrounding countryside a patchwork of stone walls, green fields, and wooded hills. The Collett estate—Killhouse, castle, shop, and cellar—stood as both refuge and target. The house itself was stout and thick-walled, built more for defense than elegance. Behind it were outbuildings, a tannery, storage cellars; before it, a yard where the smell of wet earth mingled with the musk of sheep and the iron tang of the smithy.

Mary had grown up among these smells and sounds: the clatter of hooves in the yard, the lowing of cattle, the murmur of hired men in the evenings. Her father, George Collett, was a prosperous Quaker, a man of substance with lands, mortgages, and a stubborn conscience. He had already paid his own price for faith—tithes seized, household goods taken for refusing to support the parish priest. There were stories of him standing in court, hat on, speaking plainly while bishops fumed.

Mary learned early that to be a Friend was to live with both privilege and peril. The Colletts had more than most—fields to rent, cattle to sell, a stone house when others made do with wattle and daub. But that very solidity made them a target when tempers rose. In the uneasy years after Cromwell, when old resentments smoldered,

English Protestant landholders like George were never entirely safe. A single night could bring a mob to the gate.

One winter, so the story was later told, an Irish woman who often came to Killhouse for milk overheard a plot: men planning by torchlight to storm the house, murder the family, and burn the outbuildings. Torn between loyalty to kin and gratitude for kindness, she walked the dark lane to the gate and warned them. That night, the household sat in their clothes, weapons close at hand, while the men kept watch. The attack never came—but the sense of precariousness never entirely left.

Into this world stepped Christopher Pennock, widower of Cork, already marked by prison and loss.

We don't know exactly how they met, but the circles were small: Quaker meetings at Cork and Clonmel; business ties between merchants; letters passing along the network of Friends. George Collett was wealthy, his daughter a desirable match. Christopher was no mere drifter: he was a tradesman with a shop, a man known among Friends for steadfastness if also for a certain stubbornness.

In 1672, the Cork meeting recorded the remarriage: Christopher Pennock to Mary Collett.

We can imagine their first real conversation in the courtyard at Killhouse: Mary testing this grave, plain-spoken man from Cork; Christopher noticing her quick intelligence, the way she asked pointed questions about the shop and the meeting, not just polite ones about weather and health. He would have seen at once that she was not content to be a silent ornament in some gentleman's house. She wanted to participate—in faith, in business, in the dangerous experiment of a different sort of life.

BETWEEN SHOP AND CASTLE

For a time, they moved back and forth between worlds.

In Cork, Christopher kept his shop—a narrow frontage near the harbor, where bales of cloth, coils of wire, and small goods crowded shelves and counters. The air smelled of lanolin, iron, and sea salt, with a pungent undertone of tallow from nearby chandlers. Outside, carts rattled past, and sailors shouted in half a dozen accents.

In that shop box—literally the cash drawer—churchwardens reached in and took coins "for the priest," over Christopher's protest. Once, they took seven shillings. Another time, Mary herself was hauled off to prison for refusing to close the shop on Christmas Day. It was not simply stubbornness. For Friends, those festivals were "man-made holy days," not commanded by God, and to honor them was to betray conscience. So, Mary sat in the dark at night, hearing doors slam, listening to the coughs and mutters of other prisoners, knowing that each day of absence meant lost sales and greater risk for the family.

Then back to Killhouse, where the worries were larger but the horizon wider. There, the children—Mary, Nathaniel, Joseph, Elizabeth, Ann—ran between castle and yard, half English, half Irish in their habits. They would have heard stories of raids, of Cromwell's army, of shifting loyalties. At night, wolves howled in the distance. In the day, the sound of Quaker meeting floated out of the improvised meeting room on the estate, where Friends gathered in silence under the watchful eye of local authorities.

George Collett's faith did not stay confined to piety. In 1683, he reached for something audacious: 5,000 acres in a faraway province called Pennsylvania.

A PAPER BRIDGE TO PENNSYLVANIA

In a London countinghouse—or perhaps in Cork itself—two merchants, Francis and George Rogers, unrolled a parchment bearing William Penn's seal. To Penn, these Irish Quaker merchants were not just investors; they were partners in an experiment. He needed capital to launch his "holy experiment" in Pennsylvania; they saw an opportunity in cheap land and safer refuge for Friends.

The Rogers brothers each bought 2,500 acres from Penn in 1681. Two years later, they assigned their full 5,000 acres to George Collett of Clonmel. The documents describe him as a "white tawer"— a leather dresser—of Tipperary, underscoring that his wealth came not only from rents but from skilled work.

We don't have the exact words they spoke, but the logic is clear enough. For Penn, it meant more committed Quakers with the means to settle his province and give it stability. For Collett, it meant a vast reserve of land outside the volatile politics of Ireland, a hedge against the next turn of the wheel. And for Mary and Christopher, though they may not yet have admitted it aloud, it opened the possibility of an escape hatch—a future for their children that did not depend on the goodwill of priests, sheriffs, or kings.

About a year later, Christopher and Mary acted.

THE CROSSING

The ship that carried them west was no grand vessel, just a typical 17th-century merchantman. The family boarded with trunks and chests, bedding, and a few precious tools. Somewhere among the cargo lay the legal claim that linked Killhouse to the forests of Pennsylvania.

The crossing likely took eight to ten weeks, perhaps more. Days blurred together in a weary sameness: the constant heave of the deck underfoot, the sour reek of salted beef and hard biscuit, children crying from seasickness or boredom, berths so low an adult could hardly sit upright. The air below decks grew thick and foul, damp bedding never fully dried.

At night, Mary lay awake listening to the creak of timber and the whisper of waves against the hull. When storms blew up, the lanterns swung wildly, casting crazed shadows on the beams as the ship pitched and rolled. Women clutched children. Men whispered prayers, Quaker and otherwise.

Yet there were clear days too. The older children might have been allowed on deck, hair whipped by Atlantic wind, staring at an endless blue that seemed to promise everything and nothing at once. Somewhere around week seven or eight, floating patches of seaweed signaled the approach of the American coast. Gulls appeared. Then, one morning, a darker smudge on the line between sky and sea: land.

Philadelphia was not yet the bustling city it would become. It was, in the mid-1680s, a raw place: muddy streets, scattered houses, the smell of tar and fresh-cut timber. But for Friends like Christopher, it also meant something else: a place where their worship was legal.

PHILADELPHIA: SHOP AND SORROW

Christopher did what he knew. He set up as a cardmaker and wire-drawer—making the toothed cards used to comb wool and the wire that went into them—and traded in other goods besides. His shop near the Schuylkill and the growing city center would have smelled of metal filings, oiled wood, and damp wool. Sailors came in for small items; farmers and weavers for tools and cloth; fellow Friends for necessities.

He attended Quaker meetings at the governor's house and in town. He served on small committees—investigating proposed marriages, helping settle disputes. On paper, it looked like success: land claims moving forward, business opportunities, a respected place among Friends.

For Mary, Philadelphia may have felt like a narrowing.

She had left behind the wide, green lanes of Tipperary and the safety of her father's house for a muddy grid of streets, a small wooden dwelling, and a husband more absorbed in land warrants and accounts than in the comforts of home. The children picked up strange accents; winters were bitter; summers, stifling.

We only know her feelings through the echoes in later letters, but they speak clearly enough. She was homesick. Her brothers, visiting from Ireland, saw it and fanned the flame: *You need not live like this, Mary. Father will welcome you back. Why remain in this wilderness when Killhouse still stands?*

To Christopher, it was a double betrayal. In a letter he wrote years later to Friends in Cork, he complained bitterly that his brothers-in-law had "made a difference" between him and his wife, painted him as a drunkard, drawn her affection away, and "caused her to leave me when I was sick and in distress." He remembered her promise to return in two years if life in Ireland did not prove better—and the long silence that followed instead.

Sometime around 1686, Mary left Philadelphia, taking the younger children with her back to Ireland. She never returned.

We can imagine the scene without much risk of error. The quay was crowded with barrels and bundles, ropes creaking, gulls wheeling overhead. Mary stood with Joseph, Elizabeth, Ann, perhaps Nathaniel, anxiety and resolve mixed on her face. Christopher, drawn and angry, held the hands of the children too old to cry openly but too young to understand.

"Thou knowest what thou hast promised," he might have said quietly. "Two years, and if thy father's encouragement is not as thou hopest—"

She might have looked away, eyes on the gangplank. "I cannot see the children live like this, Christopher. Father offers us a roof and plenty. I... I cannot help what my heart tells me."

"What of what thee hast promised? To Friends? To me?"

No answer that satisfied him then, or later.

As the ship pulled away, the gap between deck and quay widened, and with it the distance between Killhouse and Philadelphia. Christopher walked home alone through streets that suddenly felt more foreign than the sea.

A WEDDING AND A FORESHADOWING

In the midst of this personal wreckage, life went on.

In 1688, his daughter Sarah married William Salway, a merchant and rising provincial official. The Philadelphia meetinghouse filled with Friends as they stood hand-in-hand to recite the marriage formula: no priest, no ring, just the quiet gravity of mutual promises before God and community.

Christopher would have watched with mixed feelings: pride in his daughter's good match, sorrow that her mother and younger siblings were an ocean away, resentment that letters from Ireland were full of advice but empty of real invitation.

That same year and the years following, other currents were moving across the Atlantic—political, military, spiritual. William of Orange, James II, the looming conflicts that would culminate at the Boyne. Somewhere in that swirl of rumor and correspondence, a seed was planted: the notion that a man might fight to secure the freedoms his faith required, even if his faith forbade the sword.

Whether Christopher ever took up that sword we cannot prove. But in this first chapter of his life, we see the forces that would drive that legend: persecution, conscience, loyalty to kin, and a willingness to risk everything for a different kind of future.

In the years before the Boyne, the world in which Christopher Pennock lived had already become a narrow, grinding corridor of fear, loyalty, and whispered accusation. England no longer felt like a kingdom guided by God, but a fractured land pulled between memory and prophecy. James II sat uneasy on the English throne, a Catholic king in a country that had already fought a civil war to keep Rome at bay. For some, he was the anointed sovereign. For others, he was a warning, a shadow reaching back toward the old world they had already bled to escape.

No one breathed easily. Not in the villages of England. Not in the Quaker homes of Cork or Clonmel. And certainly not in the gatherings of Friends, where silence itself was viewed as defiance.

Christopher had long ago chosen a path outside the established order. He had been pulled from Quaker meetings, fined for the crime of worshipping differently, and imprisoned for nothing more than gathering in quiet, with others, to seek God directly. Those years had pressed sorrows into him like bruises that never quite healed. Still, he had endured. Still, he had been faithful.

Then Dorothy died.

And then Mary, though alive, was lost to him in another way—drawn back toward Ireland by her brothers, pulled by blood, by comfort, by the familiar stone estate of Killhouse at Clonmel. When she left Philadelphia, she did not simply take the children. She took the last anchor to the life he had tried to build. Christopher remained behind among strangers, the city thick with smells of leather, wool, wet wood, river water, smoke and refuse. The cobbled streets of Philadelphia, still unfinished and raw, seemed to echo his sudden aloneness.

In his letters, the hurt is still there. He did not rage so much as ache. He felt betrayed not only by her brothers, but by fate, and perhaps even by the God he had once trusted more simply.

It is in that hollowed place that the great conflict of kings took hold of him.

James and William were not merely opposing rulers; they were opposing visions of the world. James stood for continuity, hierarchy, a return toward Rome, a tightening of power. William, Prince of Orange, stood for resistance, for Protestant security, for the promise of parliamentary power over monarchy. To many Quakers, both men were only kings—and thus equally unimportant in the face of the Inner Light. But for others, especially those tangled in land, inheritance, religion, and fate, William came to represent a future that might finally leave persecution behind.

The River Boyne, then, was not chosen by chance. It was a threshold. Whoever crossed it could take Dublin. Whoever took Dublin would shape Ireland. Whoever controlled Ireland could influence the balance of power in Europe itself. The field was wet that morning with summer mist. The air carried the smell of river weeds, damp wool uniforms, horses, leather, iron. Men moved not only with orders, but with fear—fear of history, fear of God, fear that the world they knew might end before sunset.

In another life Christopher Pennock would have been nowhere near that river. He would have been in quiet meeting, hat in hand, eyes closed. But something in him had shifted. Grief had sharpened him. Abandonment had changed the weight of his convictions. He had already lost peace, lost family, lost home, and perhaps he believed he had nothing further left to lose.

So if he stood there—among William's forces, drawn in as an officer as later histories would claim—it is not difficult to imagine the conflict inside him being as fierce as the battle about to unfold. Faith on one side, fury on the other. Silence against cannon's roar. He did not fight because he loved war. If he fought, it would have been because history left him no quiet corner in which to remain. It would have been here that Christopher Pennock, as an officer, would have met Anthony Wayne, Captain and grandfather to the Major General Anthony Wayne of the American Revolution.

The victory of William at the Boyne would later be celebrated as a triumph of Protestant freedom, of constitutional government, of stability purchased through blood. But for Christopher, it would likely have felt like something more intimate: the closing of one old world and the painful beginning of another. A world in which he would return once more to Pennsylvania, not as a hopeful settler, not as a husband, but as a man marked by the turning of empires.

And when he walked again along the lands that would one day cradle Primitive Hall, lands that lay uncannily close to those of the Wayne family, it is hard not to see the threads of fate tightening. Two lines of men—Wayne and Pennock—both shaped by the same European conflict, both carried across the ocean by war, land, and belief, now rooted in the same Pennsylvania soil. Too close to be coincidence. Too precise to be ignored.

Whatever the Quaker records later chose to remember—or chose to omit—the earth itself seems to remember differently.

And it remembers him there.

CHAPTER TWO

THE LAND THAT REMEMBERED WAYNE

Before the stone house rose in Pennsylvania, before the forests fell to the axe and the Brandywine learned the sound of mill wheels, the name *Wayne* belonged to a colder, older land.

Ireland.

Not the Ireland of songs and soft rain that later centuries would imagine, but a hard-edged country of valleys and stone, of Anglican settlers and Catholic farmers pressed together under uneasy rule, of laws written in London and enforced by men who had never walked the wet fields of Wicklow.

In the years after the Battle of the Boyne, William of Orange's victory did not bring the peace all had prayed for. It brought instead a rearranging of the world. Old allegiances were torn up like weeds. New ones were planted carefully, guarded with suspicion. Veterans of William's army were rewarded with land in Ireland—not always because it was theirs by ancient right, but because it had to belong to *someone*, and William needed loyal men to hold it.

Among them was Anthony Wayne, the elder—the grandfather

of the man who would one day shake a young nation's battlefield history.

Family histories speak of him as an officer in William's service. Whether his boots sank into the wet Irish earth on the morning of the Boyne or whether he marched only in the long, nervous build-up to it scarcely matters to the soul of the story, because the war clung to him regardless. In that world, everyone carried the battle, even if they had never lifted a sword.

He settled in County Wicklow, in the quiet, resilient lands near Rathdrum and Roundwood, where the Wicklow Mountains rise and fall like the backs of sleeping giants. The air there was sharp with peat smoke and pine. In winter, the wind cut sideways. In spring, the earth smelled dark, fertile, almost sweet. Streams braided the land, cold and clear over stone.

This is where his son was born.

ISAAC WAYNE—1699

A boy who grew up with the weight of conflict still in the soil beneath his feet.

Isaac would have been a child in a landscape freshly wounded by war. Catholic and Protestant neighbors watched each other carefully. Fields changed hands with signatures made far away. Even the silence felt political. He would have heard stories—whispered or spat—of the great armies that had crossed these very hills, of fires in villages, of men who never returned from the Boyne.

And he would have learned the trade that would save him: Tanning.

It is not a poet's profession. It is a trade that smells of lime, of wet hides, of work so close and real you cannot escape it. It meant long hours by running water, scraping flesh from skin, soaking, curing, and shaping. It meant independence. It meant survival.

But in Ireland, even skill was not always enough.

By the early 1700s, the Penal Laws strangled opportunity. Land ownership for Protestants and Dissenters alike was unstable. Rents rose. Taxes crushed. The younger sons—even capable, hardworking men—had no sure inheritance and little protection.

Isaac Wayne would have felt the walls closing before there were walls.

And then, across the water, came a different voice.

WILLIAM PENN

He spoke not only of land, but of *freedom of conscience*. Of open space. Of soil that had not yet learned old hatreds. He needed farmers. He needed tradesmen. He needed men with both hands and quiet conviction.

Isaac fit the shape of that hope like a key sliding into a lock.

So in 1722, at roughly twenty-three years of age, he left the familiar stone and peat of Wicklow.

He walked away from the mountains that had watched his childhood.

He stepped aboard a ship that smelled of salt, pitch, damp rope, and fear.

The voyage would have taken six to ten weeks. Long enough for a man to replay his past again and again in the black ceiling of his berth. Long enough to imagine a future his mind had never been bold enough to draw before.

He would have listened to creaking timber and breaking waves and wondered if he would ever see land again—or if the Atlantic would swallow him like so many nameless men before him.

But it did not.

When the masts finally rested in Philadelphia's harbor, the air was thick with woodsmoke and promise. The streets were still rough, the world still young. But the land… the land listened.

Isaac moved westward into Chester County, seeking quieter ground. He purchased land—not seized it, not claimed it by blood or sword, but bought it under the Penn system, a legal path that required trust. He built. He planted. He worked.

The Wayne homestead rose from the earth. Stone stacked upon stone. A life anchored to soil for the first time in generations.

And here, in this same stretch of Pennsylvania that had drawn Christopher Pennock and would one day hold Primitive Hall, the paths of two old-world survivors converged.

Different faiths. Different wounds. The *same new world.*

Isaac raised his son there.

A boy named Anthony.

The grandson of a man touched by the Boyne.

The son of a tanner shaped by Wicklow.

A child who would grow into a name history would remember.

It is no small thing that the Pennock lands and the Wayne lands lay within the same Pennsylvania breath. No document can prove they sat at the same table or shook the same hand—but the same wind moved through their fields. The same Penn government signed the parchments. The same soil accepted their roots.

Too close to be coincidence.

Too layered to be dismissed.

The land, if it could speak, would tell you:

These men were never meant to be strangers.

And it is from this ground—this shared earth of conscience, struggle, and survival—that the next generation would rise.

A Pennock

A Wayne.

A Heacock.

Their names different, but their destinies braided together beneath the quiet, watching sky of Pennsylvania.

CHAPTER THREE

THE PEOPLE OF
THE MARSH LANE

L ong before anyone called the place "Primitive Hall," long before Joseph Pennock's brick house rose above the Brandywine (c. 1737–1740), there was another village, another cluster of timber and stone some three miles north of an old church in Staffordshire, England.

Slindon was little more than a scatter of modest farmsteads and cottages, built along a narrow, winding lane between hedgerows and fields of heavy, stubborn soil. In the low places, marsh and standing water gathered after rain. In the higher stretches, thin grass clung to the land, broken here and there by stone walls and crooked trees shaped by wind and weather.

On damp mornings, when mist gathered low over the fields, the bell of Eccleshall would toll across the countryside. Cows snorted into the cold air, birds called from the bare branches, and woodsmoke curled from clay chimneys, carrying the smell of peat, damp oak, and breakfast fires.

Somewhere in that quiet, working landscape, in the latter years of the sixteenth century (c. 1570–1600, reign of Queen Elizabeth I), the name first found its way into the parish register:

Johannes Heacocke (recorded late 1500s)

Thomasen Hacocke (recorded late 1500s)

William, son of John, of Slindon (recorded late 1500s)

Each was only a brief entry in the priest's hand, but behind the ink were lives shaped by plow, sickle, and weather. These were not men of titles or learning. They were farmers and small holders who marked the passing of time by harvest, not history. Yet, over the decades, their name appeared again and again in the records of Eccleshall, Croxton, and Sugnall Magna—through baptisms, marriages, and burials (c. 1580–1660s).

By the early seventeenth century (c. 1600–1650), families named Heacock had spread out across the surrounding countryside, intermarrying with local families bearing names such as Keene, Stacey, Meakin, and Whittington. Their lives were defined by the rhythm of the seasons, the demands of the soil, and the customs of the Church of England.

And then something began to change.

THE INWARD TURN

During the turbulent years of England's civil and religious unrest (c. 1640–1660), new ideas began to stir in the countryside—ideas carried by men like George Fox (first preaching publicly in the 1640s), who challenged the authority of the established church and spoke instead of an Inward Light, a living voice of God within the conscience of every person.

These ideas travelled on foot and by word-of-mouth, passed at markets, whispered by roadsides, exchanged in barns and cottages far from the reach of pulpits and palaces. In places like Slindon, they arrived first as rumors:

A man who would not remove his hat.

A preacher who refused titles.

A people who met in silence.

To many, it was madness. To some, it was blasphemy.

But to others—weary of hierarchy, empty ritual, and forced conformity—it was truth.

Slowly, quietly, the change took hold in families like the Heacocks. The familiar rhythms of church life began to break apart. Men and women selected silence over liturgy, conscience over ceremony. They refused to swear oaths, declined military service, rejected titles, and ceased paying tithes to priests they no longer recognized as spiritual authorities (c. 1650s–1660s).

Eventually, the parish records themselves bore witness to this transformation:

John Heacock of Slindon, a Quaker, buried at Stafford (mid- to late-1600s)

Jane Heacock, a Quaker, buried at Slindon (mid- to late-1600s)

To mark oneself as a "Quaker" in seventeenth-century England was no small act. It was an acknowledgment not only of faith, but of separation—from church, from crown, and often from the safety of the law.

BETWEEN CONSCIENCE
AND THE CROWN

Following the Restoration of Charles II (1660), Parliament passed laws specifically aimed at people such as the Quakers. Attendance at the Anglican church became compulsory. Unauthorized meetings were illegal. Refusal to take oaths brought fines and imprisonment. Repeated "offenders" could be stripped of land, goods, or liberty.

For families such as the Heacocks, faith became a dangerous daily test.

On First-day mornings, when Friends met quietly in homes rather than walking to parish worship, they did so knowing that constables or informers might be watching. A knock at the door might announce a neighbor—or the arm of the law.

For refusing to swear an oath, livestock could be seized. For declining to pay tithes, grain could be confiscated. For worshiping in silence, men could be dragged to prison, to lie in dark, overcrowded cells, suffering cold, pestilence, and hunger.

And yet, they held.

They refused to swear.

They refused to flatter.

They refused to fight.

In this same persecution (1650s–1680s), other families tied to the future story of Pennsylvania were also suffering. Christopher Pennock was imprisoned in Cork. Others were exiled or transported. A shared pressure, a shared faith, and a shared refusal to bend created a network that stretched quietly across England and Ireland.

It is within this same invisible network that the Heacocks and Pennocks first came to know of one another—not by fame, but through fellowship in suffering and conviction.

MARSH, LANE, AND
THE DECISION TO LEAVE

As the seventeenth century drew toward its close (1670s–1680s), the struggle became unsustainable. Poor harvests, religious fines, imprisonment, and the growing rigidity of English law made life unlivable for many dissenting families.

Then word came of a new place beyond the ocean.

A Quaker, William Penn, had received a charter from Charles II (1681) for land west of the Delaware River. It was a place promised to be free from religious persecution—a place where all men could worship according to the dictates of conscience.

Penn arrived in the province in October (1682), writing home:

> "The land is good, the air clear and sweet, the springs plentiful… an innumerable quantity of wild fowl and fish."

Within a few years, families known to the Heacocks—Pennock, Levis, Sharples, Pyle, Mendenhall, Chamberlin—had already crossed and taken up land in what would become Chester County. By 1693–1700 representatives of these families were serving as county officers and members of the Provincial Assembly.

The link between them was not coincidence. These were families bound together by Quaker meetings, by shared persecution, and by whispered letters passed from hand to hand across the countryside.

In Slindon, one can imagine the final conversation taking place:

"What if the ship sinks?"

"What if we stay?"

And so, the Heacocks chose the sea.

JONATHAN'S ROAD WEST

The first of the line to remain in Pennsylvania was Jonathan Heacock, the emigrant (early 1700s; likely c. 1715–1725). He boarded his ship not as a rebel but as a man compelled by faith and necessity. He carried with him the memory of England's clay soil, the toll of Eccleshall's bell, and the unbroken conviction of his Quaker conscience.

The crossing was long—eight weeks or more—in cramped berths, amidst storms, sickness, darkness, and prayer. But when land finally appeared along the Delaware, Jonathan stepped not only into a new world, but into a new identity (arrival likely c. 1715–1730).

Here, in Chester County, he found a familiar pattern reshaping itself:

> Quaker meetings at New Garden, London Grove, and Richland (established 1680s–1730s)
>
> Farms carved from forest
>
> Fields bordered by stone and oak
>
> Names that echoed those of old England

Among them stood Joseph Pennock, established by inheritance and ability (active in Chester County by c. 1716–1749), and Mary Levis Pennock, whose father had crossed from Harby, Leicestershire (late 1600s). Their families had walked the same spiritual road that Jonathan had now completed.

Also nearby stood another figure: Isaac Wayne, a fierce Protestant from County Wicklow, Ireland (emigrated late 1600s–early 1700s), whose father was said to have ridden with William of Orange at the

Boyne (1690). Though not a Quaker, he too had left a land of struggle and made his way into Penn's province.

Here, in this narrow band of Pennsylvania earth, three different paths converged.

Heacock.

Pennock.

Wayne.

Different origins—but now bound by geography, by time, and soon by blood and legacy.

THE CRESAP CRISIS AND
SHARED ALLEGIANCE (1736)

By the 1730s, Pennsylvania had grown strong enough to be threatened.

Lord Baltimore of Maryland laid claim to land settled by Penn's people, sending a ruthless frontiersman, Thomas Cresap, to stir rebellion, seize farms, and force families from their homes (c. 1730–1736). Violence threatened to erupt between colonies.

In response, Thomas Penn, son of William Penn and acting proprietor, wrote to his most trusted men—including Joseph Pennock (serving as justice and assemblyman during this period)—asking them to investigate and stop the conspiracy (November 18, 1736).

His letter spoke of:

> "… a most wicked conspiracy… in conjunction with the
> Governor of Maryland… to turn out of their houses
> and plantations… by force of arms…"

Here, again, the worlds of Pennock and Heacock overlapped—bound now not only by religion, but by political and territorial loyalty to Pennsylvania itself.

The Quakers and dissenters who had once been persecuted by kings were now defenders of a new and fragile land.

A WEB DRAWN TIGHTER (MID-1700S)

By the mid-eighteenth century (c. 1750–1770), when Joseph Pennock stood as a respected elder at "Primitive Hall" and Jonathan Heacock had long settled into American soil, their descendants had become woven into a complex fabric of families:

Sharples

Pyle

Mendenhall

Marshall

Wayne

Their lives were no longer English or Irish. They were distinctly American—bound not by crown, but by conscience, land, and memory.

The Heacocks brought the humility of smallholders who chose faith over comfort.

The Pennocks brought political will, land, and structure.

The Waynes brought martial tradition and emerging power.

Between them stretched a living human bridge—one that would soon carry a new name onto the world's stage.

That name would be Anthony Wayne (born 1745; Revolutionary service 1775–1796).

And his story begins not in a marble hall or battlefield, but among these quiet people of the marsh lane, shaped—unseen and unrecorded—by those who came before.

CHAPTER FOUR

JOSEPH PENNOCK
OF PRIMITIVE HALL

On a gray November day in 1677, in the rich Irish countryside near Clonmel, a child was born into a house that already carried more than its share of story.

He first drew breath at Killhouse, an estate outside Clonmel in County Tipperary, where his grandfather George Collett presided over a solid, comfortable Quaker household. The boy was named Joseph. In time he would sign his name *"Joseph Pennock of Marlborough"*, and generations after his death people would call him, simply, "of Primitive Hall."

But before the brick house and the title, there was the boy at Killhouse.

A CHILD BETWEEN TWO WORLDS

Joseph's early years belonged to Ireland and to his grandfather's prosperity. Killhouse was a very different world from the little Staffordshire farms of the Heacocks: a proper house with land, tenants, and connections that stretched from Clonmel to Bristol and Philadelphia.

His father, Christopher Pennock, had already made one crossing. In the 1680s, when Joseph was still a small child, Christopher carried his family to William Penn's young province. For a short time (from about 1684 to 1686) the boy lived in Philadelphia, one of the little cluster of wooden houses along the Delaware. Then his mother took him back to Killhouse. Christopher stayed on in Pennsylvania, restless, improvident, and hopeful in ways that would echo through his son's life.

So, Joseph grew up in Ireland, not in a peasant's cottage but in his grandfather Collett's home—a house where visiting Friends and traveling ministers found a welcome. One of them, the Quaker minister John Salkeld, came through the district and stayed as a guest. He met the boy and his mother there and remembered them well enough that, twenty years later, he could swear to Joseph's birth and parentage in a Philadelphia courtroom.

Killhouse was a good place to grow up: books on the shelves, horses in the stable, a sensible Quaker order to the days. But nothing in it was secure.

In 1698, George Collett died. With his death, the orbit of Joseph's life suddenly re-centered around a place he barely remembered: Pennsylvania.

From the estate records it emerged that Collett held major tracts of land in William Penn's province—part of a 5,000-acre purchase made through two brothers, William and Francis Rogers. When the accounts were settled, 3,000 acres in Pennsylvania, plus city lots in Philadelphia, fell to his grandson Joseph.

Land he had never seen, in a country he had left as a child, became the foundation of his adult life.

A FATHER'S REGRET,
AN UNCLE'S WARNING

Before Joseph left Ireland, his uncle Joseph Collett wrote to him—a letter that preserved the last bitter admission from Christopher Pennock:

> "I had a tract of land formerly in this Province that could I have kept it till this time it would have fetched me five hundred pounds without any improth, which I was fain to sell for a trifle & spent the money in misery, which if I had not done thy son and I must have suffered in time of our sickness…"

It was a father's confession across an ocean: *I had land that should have been yours. I lost it.*

The uncle went on, more practical, more pointed:

> "…we would have thee inquire & learn out when, please God, thou comest there, what tract of land this was, whether 'twas any part of the five thousand acres that was Father's lot or of the land of thy uncle George Collett's. If it be any part of those lands, we know he had not power to dispose thereof…"

In other words: *Christopher may have sold what he had no right to sell. Go and find out. Do not let your right go so.*

Then, with a touch of pastoral care that feels almost tender across three centuries, Uncle Joseph added:

> "'Twould be good for thee to have a good book with thee to read in at times, therefore would have thee buy at Bristol William Penn's *No Cross, No Crown.*"

So the young man prepared to leave: armed with a legal problem, a claim to thousands of acres, his uncle's instructions, and a recommended book on Christian self-denial.

He did not travel in peace.

CAPTURED AT SEA

Sometime around 1701–1702, Joseph booked passage from the British Isles to Pennsylvania. The Atlantic was dangerous water. France and England were rarely at rest, and the sea swarmed with privateers— half-legal predators licensed to harry enemy shipping.

Joseph's ship never made a straight course to Philadelphia.

On the way west she was taken by privateers and carried into St. Malo, on the French coast. Joseph was held there as a prisoner for about a year. Family tradition remembered "many hardships" and even a violent fight between the English sailors and their French keepers in which "the English gave the French a good drubbing."

For a young Irish Quaker gentleman, raised in Killhouse and expecting to go manage an inheritance, it must have been a rude education: sea, capture, confinement, quarrels not of his making.

Yet eventually he was released. One day the same Atlantic that had betrayed him carried him safely to the Delaware.

"THIS MAY CERTIFY…"

When Joseph finally stood again on Philadelphia soil, it was not as a boy tagging after his father but as a man with business—and a tangle of legal and family questions that had to be sorted before anything else.

He went straight to the one man he knew would remember him: John Salkeld, now in Pennsylvania.

On 2nd month 14th, 1702 (April 14, 1702) Salkeld appeared in Philadelphia and gave a formal certificate:

> "That Joseph Pennock now residing in Philadelphia is the lawful son of Christopher Pennock and Mary his wife and was born in the Kingdom of Ireland whose Mother was residing at Clonmell when I was there by which means I had the opportunity to know both the said Joseph and his Mother as also to know that Christopher the Father of the said Joseph had transported himself here at the first settling of this province and now is lately deceased, as I understand."

With that statement, Joseph's identity, legitimacy, and connection to both Ireland and Pennsylvania were firmly placed on the record. He could now act.

THE BOX OF WRITINGS

The next step was less romantic and more tedious: paperwork.

Before his death in 1701, Christopher had entrusted a box of writings—deeds, patents, leases, and assignments—to three men in Philadelphia: James Atkinson, William Southby, and Richard Sutton. These papers represented the family's right to the Rogers–Collett lands.

When Joseph asked for the box, the executors hesitated. We do not know if they were uncertain of his claim, fearful of legal trouble, or merely slow. So, Joseph did what men of his temper did: he went to law.

In a formal action, described in the surviving court record, he sued them for the deeds, patents, and other "minuments and writings." The executors appeared in person and, rather than fight, answered that they "were always ready and still are ready" to deliver everything. There in court they produced the box and handed it over.

The record closes dryly: the plaintiff "hath received the said deeds, patents & writings… Therefore the said defendants may thereof be quit."

Behind the formula, one can imagine a young man walking out of the courthouse carrying a box that contained his future:

- Indentures from William Penn to the Rogers brothers.

- Assignments from the Rogers to George Collett.

- A deed of gift from Robert Collett to Joseph and his brother Nathaniel.

- Patents to land already laid out.

With these documents in hand, he began to secure what was his.

On 12th month 22nd and 23rd, 1702, he requested warrants from the Commissioners of Property to take up the remaining balance of his 5,000 acres, "having come into this Province to look after his father's estate and the said land, and being about to return to Ireland." The records noted that because it was uncertain whether Christopher had taken up more land than the office books showed, warrants should be issued cautiously.

Even at the beginning, Joseph understood that in Pennsylvania land was both opportunity and snare. You could gain a fortune—or lose it—on the strength of a poorly worded patent.

"NOT IN UNITY WITH FRIENDS"

For all his Quaker birthright, Joseph did not at first walk "in unity" with Friends.

He dressed like a man of some means, including the fashion of a wig, a habit that disturbed one person in particular: Mary Levis, daughter of Samuel and Elizabeth (Clator) Levis of Springfield in Chester County.

Mary's parents had come over in 1684 from Harby in Leicestershire, England, and settled as respected Friends in Springfield. Samuel was a substantial "yeoman" and a man of real influence in the young colony.

Mary, like many serious young Quaker women, had doubts about men who wore wigs. She had heard that such men were "hot-tempered", too invested in fashion and pride.

So, when Joseph came to visit her father's house, Mary decided to conduct her own quiet test.

After he had gone to bed, she tiptoed into his room and hid the wig.

If Joseph was ruled by his temper, he would betray himself in the morning.

Instead, he came down calm and cheerful, his own hair carefully dressed, behaving as if nothing were amiss. Whatever she saw in his face and manner seems to have satisfied her. The story was long repeated in the family as the moment Mary decided that the man from Ireland might yet be a steady husband.

On 3rd month 3rd (May 3), 1705, in a large gathering at her father's house, Joseph and Mary spoke their marriage vows.

The record preserves the scene:

> "They, the said Joseph Pennock and Mary Levis, openly
> appeared and the said Joseph… taking the said Mary
> by the hand, declared as followeth:

> *'Be you witnesses that I take Mary Levis to be my true
> and lawful wife, promising, with God's assistance, to
> be a faithful and loving husband till death separate.'*

And the said Mary… did in like manner take the said
Joseph by the hand and declared:

> *'Be you my witnesses that I take Joseph Pennock to be
> my true and lawful husband, promising to be, with
> God's assistance, a faithful and loving wife till death
> separate.'*"

They both signed the certificate, she now as "Mary Pennock",
along with a long list of witnesses—among them Samuel and Elizabeth Levis, Jasper Yeates, Jeremiah Collett, William and Elizabeth
Shipley, and others whose names would weave through the region's
story.

Mary brought into the marriage not only character but connection. Her sister Elizabeth Levis Shipley would, a generation later,
dream of a "new land" by a wild stream and a great river, and per-
suade her husband William Shipley to settle in what was then called
Willingtown. It is because of that dream and that move that Delaware's future commercial heart, Wilmington, took shape. The Shi-
pleys built a great house there; their descendants would include
Joseph Shipley (1795–1867), partner in the English banking house
Brown, Shipley & Co.

So, in marrying Mary, Joseph linked his Irish Collett-Pennock
inheritance to a vigorous English-Quaker Levis–Shipley line that
would shape both Pennsylvania and Delaware.

MARLBOROUGH AND
THE MAKING OF AN ESTATE

After some years in Philadelphia and Bristol Township, Joseph and Mary moved west.

By 1703, 1,250 acres in what would become Marlborough Township, Chester County, had been surveyed for him—two contiguous tracts of 750 and 500 acres, laid out by surveyor Isaac Taylor. An earlier house rose there, now lost except for foundations unearthed near the public road in the garden of what would later be called Primitive Hall.

By 1710, deeds describe Joseph as "of Marlborough Township," and in 1714 the area was formally organized as West Marlborough.

In this new place, Joseph set about doing what he did best: shaping land into a working estate. On 11th month 1st, 1712/13, he petitioned for the remaining 350 acres of his 5,000-acre entitlement, stating that he and his father had already taken up 4,650. His holdings stretched from the Brandywine southward into the rolling countryside—rich land, well-watered, and heavily timbered.

By 1716, his standing among his neighbors was such that Chester County chose him to represent them in the Pennsylvania Assembly. He served again in 1719–20, 1722–24, 1726, 1729, 1732–35, and later 1743–45. The Assembly rolls list him among the Quaker leadership of the province.

The Quakers, however, watched more than public office. They watched the soul.

On 9th month 11th, 1721, New Garden Monthly Meeting recorded:

> "Joseph Pennock offered a paper… condemning his outgoing in time past from Truth and Friends and also signifying his desire to come nearer to Friends, which this meeting accepts of."

He had, in some way, wandered from strict Quaker practice—perhaps in dress, in speech, in his too-worldly involvement. Whatever the details, he felt it and returned. Friends accepted his acknowledgment and then promptly put his abilities to work.

He was named as one of the trustees who, in 1722–23, purchased ten acres on the London Tract for the use of London Grove Meeting. His name appears in the deeds as "Joseph Pennock, gentleman," alongside other trusted Friends. His father-in-law, Samuel Levis, also entrusted him with responsibility, deeding 300 acres in Springfield and Darby Townships to him and John Darby "in trust" for his wife and children.

Even his missteps were handled in the Quaker way.

On 4th month 24th, 1732, London Grove Monthly Meeting reported that "Joseph Pennock was overtaken with strong drink at Darby." Joseph, conscious of the scandal, wrote a paper condemning his own lapse; the meeting accepted his repentance and sent a copy to the Darby Friends. For a man of his stature, that admission must have cost dearly. It is one of the small, telling details that keep him human.

"MORE ADVISABLE TO RETREAT WITH SCARS..."

Land continued to require his close attention. A surviving letter, dated "Malborah ye 9th of ye 7br 1725", shows him writing to James Steel, an officer in the Proprietary land office, about a troublesome tract connected with a certain Simcock:

> "I am under some concern of mind relating to Simcock's affair... when I was at Chester I met with James Logan

who told me… that the Proprietor's family was at present so distracted or unsettled that the Commissioners know not how to form a patent or make titles to land…"

He recounts money already spent "to defend the land," but then adds, with the hard clarity of a man who has seen too much risk:

"…if I cannot have a patent, which would be my best foundation, I will quit it. For it is more advisable to *retreat with scars already received than be obliged hereafter to retreat with wounds.*

…it would be vanity in me to hazard my estate at blind-man's buff under pretense of defending a scrap of the Proprietor's."

It is a wonderfully vivid phrase: *to hazard my estate at blind-man's buff.* Joseph was no land dreamer. He would defend what he could secure; he would not be a fool for romance.

JUSTICE, ASSEMBLYMAN, NEIGHBOR

The colony recognized his reliability. On February 19, 1729, he was appointed justice of the peace for Chester County, and reappointed in 1738, 1741, 1745, and 1749. For decades, people came to him for judgments, land transactions, and the sorting of disputes that could otherwise sour a community.

By the mid-1730s, the family was firmly rooted in West Marlborough. Their eldest daughter, Elizabeth, married Edward Tatnall at London Grove Meeting on 4th month 11th, 1735; among the signers of their marriage certificate were Elizabeth's aunt Elizabeth Shipley and William Shipley of Willingtown, soon to build their great house on the Delaware.

Their eldest son, Samuel, reached his majority, and on May 10, 1737, Joseph and Mary, "for natural love and affection," deeded him 402½ acres from the Marlborough tract. He then requested a certificate from New Garden Meeting to transfer to Philadelphia Meeting, where he intended to settle and marry Elizabeth Widdifield. Mary wrote plainly to the Philadelphia Friends:

> "This may acquaint you that I do give my free consent to my son Samuel to proceed on the account of marriage with his friend Elizabeth Widdifield…"

The family was growing outward: a daughter to Willingtown and the Delaware, a son to Philadelphia as a carpenter, others remaining closer to the home place.

In the midst of all this, Joseph turned to a project that would define his memory.

"THE SAME YEAR I BUILT MY NEW HOUSE"

In his Bible Concordance—the same book that held the family record—Joseph made a simple note:

> "The 14th of the 9th 1738 then my impostum broke and the same year I built my new house."

The "impostum" was an abscess; its bursting marked the end of a serious illness. That same year, recovering his health, he completed the building of a large brick house on his West Marlborough land.

Today it is known as Primitive Hall.

The house was ambitious for its time and place: thick brick walls, inside and out, laid in Flemish bond; a wide central hallway paved in brick; paneled wainscoting climbing the staircase; paneled overmantels above deep fireplaces; high ceilings; and simple but finely proportioned chair rails.

Tradition held that Joseph himself selected the timber for the interior from his own woods. The joinery was pegged; cupboards were hung on "butterfly" hinges; doors were fitted with sturdy iron latches.

Within those walls stood the furniture that can still be traced to his ownership:

- A wainscot settles along the wall.
- A great walnut gate-leg table.
- A desk where deeds were drawn and letters written.
- Sturdy chairs, some of them now in museums or private collections.
- A Rittenhouse clock, marking time in the hall.
- A small spice chest, whose drawers would carry the faint, lasting aroma of nutmeg and clove.

In that house, as one later writer put it, "Joseph held court." A room in the basement served as a lockup for prisoners brought before him as justice. Friendly Native Americans came and went; the doors, tradition says, "were never locked" against them. Members of the Assembly visited and stayed; public matters were discussed beside his own hearth.

Here, in the deep forest of Chester County, the private life of a Quaker patriarch and the public life of the province met.

THE CRESAP AFFAIR:
DEFENDING THE PROVINCE

One of the clearest glimpses we get of Joseph in his public role comes from a tense frontier episode in 1736.

The boundary between Pennsylvania and Maryland was still unsettled. The Maryland proprietors, led by Lord Baltimore, claimed land that Pennsylvanians had settled. To press their claim, they used a rough frontiersman named Thomas Cresap, who tried by force to drive German settlers off their farms.

Thomas Penn, son of William and then in Philadelphia as proprietor, recognized the danger. On November 18, 1736, he wrote to five trusted men of Chester County—Joseph Brinton, Caleb Cowpland, Joseph Pennock, William Webb, and John Taylor:

> "As a most wicked conspiracy hath been lately discovered to be carried on by several of the inhabitants of your county in conjunction with the Governor of Maryland, with intention by force of arms to turn out of their houses and plantations the persons and families of more than fifty of His Majesty's subjects inhabiting this province...

I have thought proper to desire that you would do this acceptable service to your country as well as to myself..."

Penn urged them to go to the house of William Miller, question those involved, and identify leaders who might need to be committed "as disturbers of the peace" until security could be had.

The letter went to Primitive Hall, where Joseph, already aging but still vigorous, took up the task. It was a far cry from Killhouse and even from the St. Malo prison. The man who had once sought shelter under Penn's charter now acted as defender of Penn's province against outside aggression.

It is not hard to see in this episode one of the threads that will lead, in the next chapter, to Anthony Wayne—frontier fighter, defender of Pennsylvania's western line, and heir, in a very different style, to the work men like Joseph had begun.

SORROW, ADJUSTMENT, AND THE LONG DUSK

Life in a large Quaker family brings as many sorrows as joys.

On 1st month 1747/8, after more than four decades of marriage, Mary (Levis) Pennock died. She had served as an overseer at London Grove Preparative Meeting; after her death, Mary Taylor was named to that role. Mary left behind a house full of memories and a husband now well into his seventies.

Joseph, however, continued to order his affairs.

He had already made an informal will in June 1740 during a serious illness, carefully dividing his lands among sons and providing for his daughters by portions and annuities. After he recovered, he confirmed and adjusted his gifts by deed:

- January 20, 1742: he and Mary confirmed their earlier gift of 500 acres on the south side of the Brandywine to their son William.

- November 12, 1744: they deeded 420 acres in Marlborough Township to Joseph Jr., "for one shilling and natural love and affection."

- Earlier, in 1739, their son Nathaniel had received 492½

acres in West Marlborough on the south side of the "street," adjoining the London Tract and Caleb Pusey's land, with attached ground rents and obligations.

The children themselves formed a small community around him:

1. Elizabeth, married Edward Tatnall, living at Wilmington (Willingtown).

2. Samuel, a carpenter in Philadelphia.

3. William, of the Brandywine tract.

4. Mary, who died young.

5. Nathaniel, of West Marlborough.

6. Joseph Jr., of East/West Marlborough.

7. Alice, who married into other local families.

8. Anne, born 6th month 6th, 1718, who did not marry.

9. Sarah, born 9th month 24th, 1720, who would marry into the Marshall family.

10. Hannah (12th month 24th, 1722—7th month 17th, 1779), who married Jacob Marshall, brother of the botanist Humphry Marshall; they had no issue.

11. Levis, born 11th month 31st, 1725, who would become heir to Primitive Hall.

12. Susanna, born 1st month 28th, 1728, who married Isaac Evans and tragically died with her only child.

As the years advanced, Joseph's world narrowed physically but remained connected intellectually and politically.

In 1764, John Morton—younger colleague in the Assembly and future signer of the Declaration of Independence—wrote from Ridley:

> "Sir, I am prevailed on in favour of my kinsman Mr. Philip Ford... to trouble you with this epistle...
>
> Notwithstanding you have not troubled yourself to attend elections some years past, yet your interest, respect, and opinion about home, when opportunity suits, may do him service... I can assure you from my acquaintance with him that his principles are honest..."

Morton appeals directly to Joseph's "age and character", knowing that in his "quarter" of the county, his opinion still carried weight.

That same year, a letter came from much farther away—from Clonmel, the town of his youth.

His cousin Stephen Collett wrote on June 21, 1764, claiming that his father Robert (Joseph's uncle) had been entitled to 500 acres of Pennsylvanian land originally purchased by George Collett, and alleging that Joseph had unlawfully "possessed himself" of it. Robert, he said, had refused to settle the land on Joseph, but Joseph had taken it anyway.

It was a sharp accusation, made across an ocean.

Joseph's reply, dated Philada 18th of the 10th mo 1764, is calm, precise, and quietly firm. He outlines the facts:

- George purchased 500 acres.
- George died intestate and without issue; by law the land descended to his eldest brother Robert (Stephen's father).

- Robert, by deed dated 9 November 1696, assigned all his right and title to his nephews Nathaniel and Joseph Pennock, their heirs and assigns forever.

- Christopher, as administrator, had sold the land to "a Dutchman" approximately sixty-six years ago.

He enclosed an exemplification of the deed for Stephen's satisfaction and concluded:

> "…upon the whole thou wilt find thy claim ungrounded; hadst thou any right, justice should be done thee… thy letter was the first I ever received, and now answer it fully, wishing thee and thy family peace and prosperity. I am thy esteemed and affectionate kinsman."

It is hard to imagine a more Pennock-like answer: factual, courteous, final.

In a small memorandum book, his son Nathaniel recorded everyday kindnesses to his aging father:

> "1768 Father had a quarter of sugar… stuff for coat, jacket, and breeches with trimmings… to Doctor Bass…
>
> 1770 bought for Father 2 lb of chocolate, 3 licorice sticks… 2 ounces aloes, one of saffron, one of myrrh…"

Sugar, cloth, medicine, chocolate. The items of a long old age, supported by dutiful children.

THE LAST WILL AND THE GAZETTE

At last, in his mid-nineties, Joseph set his affairs in final order.

On 10th month 28th, 1770, "sick and infirm in body, but through the mercy of the Lord of a sound and well-disposing mind and memory," he executed his last will.

He began by confirming what he had already done:

> "Whereas I have already settled and promoted most of my children by considerable donations of lands and other effects, namely my eldest son Samuel, William, Nathaniel, and Joseph, and my daughter Elizabeth, now I do hereby ratify and confirm all those particular donations…"

He then:

- Gave £20 to his daughter Elizabeth Tatnall, and £10 each to her four children, Mary, Joseph, Elizabeth, and Sarah.

- Ordered that a £12 annual rent from 400 acres in Kennett Township go to his son Nathaniel, on condition that Nathaniel pay £50 to his daughter Sarah Marshall and that the annuity be charged with it.

- Left £100 from the residuary estate to Sarah Marshall.

- Devised Primitive Hall and its 700 acres to his son Levis, "the messuage and plantation whereon I now dwell… be it more or less," together with "all utensils, gears, tools, and implements of husbandry," and all his plate, household goods, and furniture, except one best feather bed for Nathaniel.

- Left to Levis "one set of the works of Thomas Story and all my physical books."

- Left to Nathaniel "the works of William Penn and all my books treating of husbandry."

- Forgave the bond of his late eldest son Samuel by directing that any money due on the bond of 24th of 1st month 1752 be considered as a legacy to Samuel's sons Joseph and Samuel, provided they execute a general release of any further claim on his estate.

- Ordered that the residue of his goods and credits be divided into four equal parts—three parts to his sons Nathaniel, Joseph, and Levis, and the fourth part to the youngest sons of his late son William: William, Caleb, Samuel, and Joshua, equally. He noted plainly that to his son Samuel he had "in his life time given more than a child's portion."

He named Nathaniel and Levis as his executors.

When Joseph Pennock died on March 28, 1771, in the ninety-fifth year of his age, the Pennsylvania Gazette carried his obituary on April 11, 1771, on the same page as news of fleets sailing from Cadiz, troop movements near Gibraltar, and the strained finances of France. Amid that global news, Philadelphia readers saw this:

> "On the 28th ult. died JOSEPH PENNOCK, Esq., of Upper Marlborough, in Chester County, one of the people called Quakers, in the 95th year of his age. He came into this Province when he was about 20 years old, and was very early in life chosen one of our Representatives,

in which capacity he served his Country with ability and integrity… After continuing many years a valuable Member of the Assembly, he retired from public business with the esteem of all who knew him.

In his private life, few have equalled, and hardly any excelled him…

He had acquired by reading and conversation with gentlemen of the faculty a considerable knowledge in physic—this he employed frequently for the advantage of his friends, acquaintance, and more especially the poor, without any pecuniary reward…

Temperance, joined with hospitality, ever graced his board… He had a natural politeness and sweetness of manners that irresistibly attracted respect and love from all: he indeed had the happy art which very few attain to, 'who laughing, could instruct.'

…To crown the whole of this exemplary patriarch's character, he lived the Christian from his youth to his exit."

His inventory, taken April 18, 1771, makes the obituary almost tangible:

- A clock and case—£18

- A desk—£2

- A "close press"—£1

- "½ Doz black chairs & armed ditto"—19s

- "3 pewter dishes & a bed pan"—£2

- Two large walnut tables—£4-10s

- A "case of drawers with a frame"—£3-10s

- Several beds with their coverings, chests, and chairs.

His books were divided into two lists:

Willed

- Works of William Penn, 2 vols.—£1-10s

- "Agriculture," 2 vols.—£1

- Works of Thomas Story

- "Physical books," "Herbill," and "small books"—together £3-17s-6d

Not willed

- "Rallegh and Josephas"—£2

- "A Bible &—"—£2

- Other "small books"—£2-7s-3d

The total estate appraised came to £988-12s-1¼d. For the end itself, the expenses were modest:

- £1-15s to Joseph Pyle for the coffin.

- 5 shillings to Francis Lamborn for digging the grave.

- An allowance of three gallons of wine, costing £2-19s-6d, "for funeral expenses."

In 1774, his sons Nathaniel and Levis filed their account as executors, showing receipts and legacies paid: to Elizabeth Tatnall and her children, to Sarah Marshall and her husband Humphry, to Samuel's line, and for goods "willed to Levis" and to Nathaniel. The total—just over £1,050—closed the ledger on nearly a century of life.

THE SHADOW HE CAST

Joseph and Mary (Levis) Pennock's children spread out across Chester County, Philadelphia, and Delaware. Their marriages linked them to families we have already met: Tatnall, Marshall, Pusey, Evans and others. Their lands marched along the same roads and ridges as those of the Heacocks and the Waynes.

By the time the Gazette printed Joseph's obituary in 1771, a boy who had grown up not far away—Anthony Wayne, born 1745 at Paoli—was already a young man of twenty-six, restless, ambitious, and shaped by the same Chester County fields Joseph had fenced and measured.

In Primitive Hall, bookshelves still held the works of William Penn and Thomas Story. On the mantle, perhaps, the Rittenhouse clock still ticked. Outside, fields once cleared by Joseph's tenants and sons lay under cultivation. Farther down the road, the Waynes' tannery and farm were molding the character of a future general.

All of them—Pennock, Heacock, Wayne—moved now in the same settled landscape Joseph had done so much to create: a fabric of farms, meetings, courts, and quiet Quaker influence.

In that fabric, Primitive Hall remained what it had been from the year Joseph's abscess broke and his "nu house" rose from the brick kilns—a solid center of gravity in a changing world. This esteemed home still stands today.

The life of Joseph Pennock establishes the wealth and influence of the family. Worlds apart from future ancestors of this family, yet integrally tied to the history of the past. It would be through the bloodline of his son William and William's grandson that the Pennock family connects to the life of Jane Pennock and her daughters Susannah Clarissa and Nancy Hemtrietta.

In the next chapter, we will turn from the Quaker patriarch's hall to the house of a different kind of patriarch: the Waynes of Paoli, whose descendant would carry Pennsylvania's story onto battlefields far beyond the Brandywine.

CHAPTER FIVE

BEFORE THE BLACK SNAKE CAME

Before the echo of axes, before the ring of iron on timber, before the name "Defiance" had ever been whispered by a soldier or scratched into a map, there was only the land.

And the land was old.

At the forks of the Maumee and the Grand Glaize, the forest pressed in from every direction, an immense living cathedral whose vaulted canopy dimmed the sun even at midday. Trunks of beech, oak, sycamore, and ash rose like pillars from a floor of moss, rotting leaves, and black mud that swallowed the foot whole. Fog clung to the underbrush. Birds called from invisible perches. Now and then a deer stepped between the shadows, ears alert, breath forming silver threads in the early light.

The two rivers met in silence.

The Maumee moved with the steady patience of a river that had carved its path long before any tribe or nation named it. Broad, strong-shouldered, carrying the weight of northern waters, it glided between clay banks that sloped into marsh grass and reeds. The Grand Glaize was more modest—a quiet river, shallow and slow, its voice barely more than a murmur as it slid through the low ground. It did not roar. It did not rise with power. It crept, winding its way through the soft flatlands where the swamp began.

Here, the Great Black Swamp breathed.

It stretched for miles—an enormous, waterlogged wilderness of quagmire and willow thickets, where a man could wander a day and travel only half a mile. Mosquitoes rose in black clouds. Frogs sang in an endless chorus. Fallen logs, soft as sponge, lay half-submerged in dark pools that reflected nothing but the green shadow of the canopy.

The tribes called the confluence a meeting of paths—roads of water, roads of forest, roads of migration. Long before white men spoke of it, the place served as council ground, hunting ground, and crossroad. Ottawa, Shawnee, Miami, and Delaware paddled quietly along the rivers, their canoes slipping through the reeds like moving shadows. Fur traders—French, mostly—passed through as early as the 1600s, their paddles steady, their loads heavy with pelts, their fires flickering along the banks at night.

Some nights the glow of a single lodge fire reflected against low clouds; other nights the swamp swallowed all light, leaving the rivers to whisper to one another in the dark.

It was a place of profound stillness, yet no traveler ever mistook that stillness for peace.

The forest watched.

The swamp listened.

And the tribes—who knew these shadows by heart—waited.

THE MURMUR OF CHANGES

By the late eighteenth century, rumors carried themselves along the ancient paths:

A new army is coming.

A new kind of soldier.

A general whose mind moves like a snake through grass.

They called him Shamokin Skenandoah's name for him first—"Black Snake"—not for his color, but for his motion. A creature who only struck with intent, who wound himself through the land with patience, who studied every bend of river and every twist of trail before revealing his bite.

The Great Black Swamp had swallowed many armies.

It had broken supply lines.

It had punished haste.

It had turned muskets to rust and wagons to splinters.

Yet word spread that this new general was different.

He watched.

He learned.

He adapted.

He had come from Fort Greene Ville, south through forest and rain, reorganizing a shattered force into something the tribes began to fear.

And he was heading north—toward the dark heart of the forked rivers.

Toward the place that would one day be Defiance.

A LAND WAITING FOR FIRE

As midsummer (1794) approached, humidity thickened the air above the Maumee. Storm clouds built theatrically over the distant treeline, their edges stitched with lightning. Wolves hunted in the cool hours, their paws silent on the damp earth. Near the Grand Glaize, a trader lifted his head, sensing something in the change of wind—a tremor, faint but definite, like the far-off drum of hooves.

A scouting party of Miami hunters paused along a ridge, listening for the same sound. One elder nodded, his voice hushed.

"The Black Snake comes," he said.

"And he brings the storm with him."

What none of them knew was how quickly the land itself would change.

That the quiet confluence, wrapped in vines and shadow, would soon be carved open by axes.

That the first ring of a hammer against a felled timber would echo across the swamp like a prophecy.

That a fort—intimidating in structure, defiant, angular as a clenched fist—would rise on that sacred ground within days.

And that when it stood complete, its builder would utter the words:

> "I defy the English, the Indians, and all the devils of
> hell to take it."

Only then would the place finally earn its name.

THE BLACK SNAKE ARRIVES

The sound reached the rivers before the soldiers did.

A low, rhythmic pounding—distant, then nearer. Hooves.

Hundreds of them. Then the clatter of iron-bound wheels striking roots and stone. A murmur of voices, boots sinking into the mud of old buffalo paths. Birds startled from the trees. Deer bolted through the underbrush. Even the frogs fell silent.

The Black Snake had entered the swamp.

General Anthony Wayne rode near the front, his posture rigid, his jaw set in the stern line of a man who had learned patience the hard way. He had seen armies break before. His own countrymen had faltered at St. Clair's defeat, their blood spilled across the very forests he was now crossing. But Wayne had rebuilt them—drilled them until their muskets rose as one, taught them how to move through trees as silently as their enemies, hardened them until they no longer feared this land.

Behind him stretched the Legion of the United States, a strange new force—part infantry, part cavalry, part frontier scouts—disciplined enough to march in formation, flexible enough to melt into the wilderness when the trail narrowed to a single muddy track.

Mud sucked at the soldiers' boots. Clouds of insects rose in torment. Wagons bogged down and had to be lifted by hand. Axes rang as trees were felled to clear a path wide enough for cannon wheels.

Yet Wayne pressed forward.

"Slow is smooth," he told his officers, "and smooth is fast."

The men repeated it quietly, the words becoming a rhythm that matched the creak of leather and the groan of wagon timber.

THE CONFLUENCE REVEALED

When the army finally reached the high ground between the two rivers, Wayne halted.

Before him lay the confluence—an ancient meeting place, a natural fortress carved not by men but by centuries of water and wind. The Maumee spread wide and bright beneath the summer sun, its surface dappled with shifting reflections from clouds above. The Grand Glaize wound toward it like a shy tributary seeking the embrace of its larger sister.

For a long moment, Wayne said nothing.

His officers waited, the only sound the hum of swamp insects and the distant cry of a hawk circling overhead.

Then Wayne's eyes narrowed—not in fear, but in understanding. "This," he said, "is the place."

AXES IN THE WILDERNESS

The command spread down the lines:

Make camp.

Prepare tools.

Begin the work.

If the forest had watched the army's approach, it now felt the blow of its presence.

Men swung axes in relentless rhythm, the echoes ringing through miles of timber. Great oaks toppled. Pines crashed into thickets. Saplings were hauled away and lashed into makeshift scaffolds. Fires burned constantly as brush was cleared, the smoke drifting over the rivers like gray veils.

Wayne designed the fort himself—a presence of being defiant. It would not hide within the forest. It would dominate it.

Bastions rose first, their points aimed like spearheads. Then log walls, each timber squared by hand. Trenches were dug deep and lined with sharpened stakes. Platforms for artillery took shape under the calloused hands of carpenters. The smell of hewn timber mixed with sweat, horses, and river mud.

Night fell, but the work did not stop. Torches flickered along the construction lines. Hammering continued under the glow of firelight. Soldiers' silhouettes rose and fell, shadows cutting across the clearing like moving ghosts.

The tribes watched from the forest edge.

Silent. Unseen. But not unafraid.

For they had never witnessed anything like this—a fort rising in mere days, its walls broad enough to shelter hundreds, its guns positioned to command both rivers and all the land between.

NAMING THE PLACE

On a humid afternoon, when the walls stood nearly complete and the soldiers had begun to cut firing ports into the timber, Wayne climbed the highest bastion and looked out over the wilderness.

The men below paused long enough to hear his voice carry on the heavy air:

> "I defy the English, the Indians, and all the devils of
> hell to take this place."

His officers exchanged glances.

The soldiers murmured.

The forest held its breath.

The name settled instantly, as if it had always existed.
Fort Defiance.

AFTER THE BATTLE

Only weeks later, Wayne would fight the Battle of Fallen Timbers—swift, decisive, shattering the last great coalition of tribes who had resisted American expansion. When he returned to the fort, victorious, he found it standing exactly as he had left it: solid, unyielding, commanding the land like a king over his domain.

The tribes who had once controlled these waterways retreated westward under the terms of the Treaty of Greene Ville. Traders began to pass more freely. Soldiers came and went. Hunters drifted through. Settlers—careful at first—followed the path Wayne had cut.

The world was changing.

THE FORT THAT BECAME A TOWN

For two decades, the location of Fort Defiance remained a landmark—sometimes garrisoned, sometimes quiet, always imposing. Travelers used it as a meeting point. Fur traders stored their packs near its walls. Surveyors marked its location as the anchor for new parcels of land being opened to settlement.

Then came the War of 1812.

The old fort, weathered and weary, was no longer enough. A new fort rose upriver on the Au Glaize—Fort Winchester, built under the orders of General William Henry Harrison. Its log walls stood near where the Maumee narrowed, its presence a shield against British forces pushing from the north.

Gunfire echoed across the rivers.

Supply wagons rumbled through the mud.

Messengers rode day and night.

When peace finally returned, the forts fell silent—but the land no longer would.

CHAPTER SIX

WILLIAM C. HOLGATE

THE SLOW BIRTH OF A CITY

By the 1820s, the name "Fort Defiance" lingered mostly in stories. The Army had moved on. The tribes had been forced farther west. The Great Black Swamp still strangled the land, but settlers trickled in, draining fields, hacking roads through the mire, planting corn where soldiers once drilled.

And then came a young Vermonter named William C. Holgate.

Where others saw wilderness, Holgate saw potential. He purchased land near the old fort, laid out streets, coaxed merchants to build shops, and enticed mills and factories to settle along the rivers. He recorded everything in his journal—muddy streets, disputes over land, the smell of sawdust from new mills, the promise of the canal.

Holgate was a builder, a persuader, a man who could imagine a city long before one existed.

And slowly—very slowly—his vision took shape.

The Miami and Erie Canal was dug through forest and swamp.

Packet boats began to arrive.

Commerce blossomed.

Families arrived—Blairs, Ilers, Heacocks, Hamiltons—drawn by the promise of land and work.

The swamp receded.

The rivers grew busier.

The smell of pine and mud gave way to the smell of sawdust, lime mortar, wet wool, and horses.

Defiance was no longer a lonely clearing in the wilderness.

It was becoming a town.

HOLGATE'S VISION

William C. Holgate walked the ground like a man who could see layers of time invisible to everyone else.

When he first arrived in northwest Ohio in the mid-1830s—a young attorney from New York with boots still too clean for the swamp—the land must have seemed almost indifferent to him. The confluence of the Maumee and Auglaize lay quiet under its veil of mist. Trees leaned over the water as if listening. The few cabins scattered near the old fort weathered each season with tight-lipped resignation.

To most men, the place looked forgotten.

Holgate was not most men.

He carried a journal wherever he went, its leather worn smooth from constant use. Lay it open and the pages breathed with his restless imagination:

> *"Good soil. Thick timber. Water enough for mills. A future town here—if one is stubborn enough."*

The swamp tried to intimidate him. Mud swallowed boots. Mosquitoes rose in clouds thick as smoke. Horses balked at the sinking earth. The summers steamed like a kettle left too long on the fire, and the winters could freeze a man stiff before he reached the next cabin.

Holgate endured every bit of it.

He learned the rivers first. The Maumee was the queen—broad, muscular, moody. The Auglaize, shallow and slow in summer, was no more than a shy tributary then—*nothing* like the churning force it would later become during floods and canal overflows. The Tiffin River (once called Bean Creek to its north) twisted relentlessly through low ground, a stubborn ribbon that refused to straighten itself for the convenience of men.

Surveyors scratched their heads, traders shrugged, and most settlers kept to higher ground.

But Holgate walked the banks and felt possibility humming beneath the mud.

A POLITICIAN OF THE FRONTIER

The people of old Williams County—of which Defiance was then only a tiny corner—were a suspicious lot. They distrusted newcomers, especially those who carried books rather than axes.

Holgate won them over anyway.

Not with force.

Not with threats.

But with listening.

He knew every miller by name, every matron who mourned a husband lost to malaria, every veteran who still remembered the crack of muskets near Fort Winchester. He walked the roads at dusk, pausing by cabin doors, absorbing the wants and fears of those who had sunk their lives into this land.

When he rose in meetings—lean, sharp-featured, his voice steady—they listened.

"Defiance has more future in a single square mile," he once said, "than other towns have in their entire county."

By the 1840s he had enough influence to attempt something bold—something that would reshape the map itself.

CARVING DEFIANCE
OUT OF THE FRONTIER

In Holgate's mind, Defiance was the heart of the region.

In reality, it was a neglected outpost at the southern edge of Williams County.

Williams County was vast—too vast. Residents complained that the courthouse was too far, that roads were too few, that their voices were lost behind the louder settlements of Bryan and Montpelier.

Holgate seized the moment.

He rallied the settlers of the Maumee valley, standing on stumps, front porches, tavern tables—anywhere he could find a crowd. He pointed to the rivers, to the newly platted streets, to the rising mills.

"Why," he asked, "should this place not be the seat of its own county?"

Men nodded. Women whispered agreement. Surveyors unrolled maps.

And slowly, the idea took shape.

In the mid-1840s—after petitions, assemblies, and fierce arguments in the General Assembly—Defiance County was carved out of Williams County, its boundaries drawn around the confluence like lines on a destiny long delayed.

Holgate's fingerprints were on every decision.

THE CANAL THAT
CHANGED EVERYTHING

Even Holgate, with all his imagination, could not have built Defiance without the canal.

The Miami and Erie Canal had been approved in 1837, though money slowed everything and the digging took place in fits and starts. Speculation raged across northwest Ohio. Men in Brunersburg, betting that the canal would favor their little settlement along the Tiffin River (Bean Creek), built mills, shops, and houses in anticipation of becoming a major exchange point.

Speculators drew lots on maps that were little more than guesses. Holgate watched quietly.

He visited the state engineers. He studied soil. He rode with surveyors. He understood something the others didn't:

The confluence, not Brunersburg, was the true hinge between north and south, east and west.

And so the canal—after much political maneuvering and engineering debate—did not follow the Tiffin's uncertain, twisting path.

It anchored itself in Defiance.

When the ditch fill was completed in 1843, and the first packet boats slid past the newly built mule bridge west of the Clinton Street river crossing, the town awakened.

The canal widened behind the row of wooden storefronts like a second street of water. Warehouses rose. A sawmill buzzed from dawn to dusk. Tailors, grocers, carpenters, and tavern keepers multiplied. The smell of wet mule rope, river mud, fresh lumber, and grain mixed into the perfume of a rising town.

And into this came the Heacocks and Hamiltons—some as travelers, some as workers, some as dreamers—pulled by the new artery pulsing through what had once been a quiet corner of the wilderness.

THE RAILROADS
CONFIRMED THE FUTURE

Canals brought life.

Railroads brought ambition.

Holgate knew that towns lived or died by transportation lines, and he fought like a man possessed to secure them.

The Wabash, St. Louis & Pacific Railroad was his first triumph.

The Baltimore & Ohio Railroad followed—so significant that a new town in nearby Henry County was named Holgate in gratitude.

Tracks hammered into the ground like promises.

Steam whistles pierced the valley.

Timetables replaced guesswork.

And Defiance became, unmistakably, a city.

THE PLATFORM FOR THE HEACOCKS

All of this—the canal, the railroads, the county seat, the rising stores and inns—created the perfect conditions for the success that would follow.

When the Heacocks arrived, they did not come to wilderness.

They came to a place that Holgate had already imagined, fought for, and lifted from mud to commerce.

A place where travelers needed lodging.

Where wagoners needed food.

Where packet boat crews needed beds.

Where railroad workers needed whiskey and warmth.

A place where a determined family could build not just a house, but a business,

and from that business --

A legacy.

THE LAND THAT WAITED

By the time the canal boats began gliding through the new locks in the 1840s, Defiance no longer resembled the lonely outpost General Anthony Wayne had carved from the wet earth half a century earlier.

The Black Snake of the frontier—Wayne himself—had long since faded into memory, his fort abandoned to vine and silence. Yet something of him remained, woven invisibly into the place. You could feel it at dusk, when fog rose from the Maumee and wrapped the old fort site in coils of silver, like smoke curling from a campfire no one had tended in generations. The land still held the echo of drums, the thud of axes, the murmuring cadence of his men digging through nights thick with the smell of pine sap and damp soil.

And though Wayne never saw what the place would become, it was his fort that first interrupted the vast solitude of the Great Black Swamp.

His ramparts turned the wilderness into a destination.

His presence made maps bend toward the confluence.

His name gave the place a story before it ever had a future.

The swamp tried to reclaim it after he marched away. Trees crept down the slopes. Canoes slipped past without stopping. Traders still came, but fewer each year. Then came Harrison and the War of 1812, the brief revival of Fort Winchester, the smoke of musket fire drifting once more through the tree line. And then again—quiet.

Until Holgate arrived.

Holgate, who could sense promise under mud.

Holgate, who saw a town where others saw a clearing.

Holgate, who would not surrender the land to obscurity.

It was his stubbornness that saved Defiance from becoming nothing more than a parenthetical in a history of vanished forts. First came the canal: mule bells jingling in the dawn, packet boats slipping past storefronts whose windows glowed with lamplight, the slow heartbeat of commerce pulsing through the watery spine of the town. Then the railroads brought a new rhythm—steel on steel, the high wail of steam whistles bending over the rooftops, the future roaring into being on iron rails.

By the time the first Hamiltons and Heacocks reached the Maumee valley, Defiance was no longer a rough encampment of fallen trees and muddy boots.

It was a rising point on the map—

a place of mills and warehouses,

of taverns filled with wagoners' laughter,

of canal men shouting from towpaths,

of sawdust drifting from furniture factories,

of ironworks clanging through open doors,

of women carrying baskets of laundry to the riverbank,

of children running along planks laid beside the locks.

It was a town with its own gravity.

A town built from the layered ambitions of men who had worked far beyond their own lifetimes—Wayne, Harrison, Holgate—each shaping the land in turn, each leaving something sturdy enough for the next generation to stand upon.

And it was into this town, this confluence of rivers and destinies, that the Heacocks would soon bring their quiet industry…and the Hamiltons their iron-dusted hopes.

The roads were ready.

The waterway was open.

The rails gleamed like a promise.

The land itself was waiting.

CHAPTER SEVEN

THE HAMILTON'S OF IRELAND

THE LEAVING OF ARMAGH

Before Kirks Mills, Pennsylvania, echoed with the splash of Octoraro Creek against the mill wheel—before the hiss of steam, the bite of iron, or the scent of wet oak entered the Hamilton story—there was a different world across the ocean. It was a world of low stone walls and sodden fields, of crooked lanes pressed between thorn hedges, of peat smoke drifting across the moors of County Armagh.

This was the first home the Hamiltons remembered.

Their village was small enough that every voice carried from one cottage to the next. A handful of dwellings clung to a winding lane where the morning fog pooled between hedgerows, and a millrace cut a narrow line through the fields before spilling over a wooden wheel that groaned and creaked in every season. Even on still days, you could hear the deep murmur of falling water, as steady as breath.

The Hamilton cottage stood among these few homes, modest but strong, its door opening into the workshop where generations of Hamilton men had shaped wood and iron. The scents inside shifted with the work—fresh-cut oak one day, hot metal the next, the tallow smoke of a small forge rising through roof beams blackened by years of labor.

The Hamiltons were not grand craftsmen, but their skill carried weight. They carved gears with careful hands, shaped axles from cherry-hot iron, and raised millstones with rigs of rope and timber they built themselves. They understood how water spoke to wood, how torque traveled through a turning shaft, how one misplaced tooth could throw an entire mill into ruin. Their livelihood depended on precision, and so it became their language.

The sound of their workshop was answered by another just across the lane.

The Stevensons, linen weavers by tradition, lived in a cottage warmed by loom-clatter and the rustling whisper of flax. Their looms chattered through winter and well past dusk, the rhythm of their work blending with the Hamilton hammers until no one in the village could tell where one craft ended and the other began. A Stevenson boy might carry a newly planed beam from the Hamilton shop to brace a loom; a Hamilton lad might deliver flax boards to the Stevenson porch. The families traded tools, traded stories, traded labor. In hard seasons, they traded survival.

Somewhere in those years of shared hardship and shared hearth fire, Hamilton blood mingled with Stevenson blood. Perhaps a Hamilton daughter married a Stevenson son, or a Stevenson girl fell in love with a Hamilton craftsman. No parish minister ever wrote the truth into a neat line in a book. But the kinship endured—woven in memory, in proximity, in the quiet certainty that the two families belonged to one another.

Yet life in Armagh carried more than craft and companionship.

It carried tension.

The Hamiltons were Presbyterians in a land governed by others. They tithed to churches not their own, held leases at the mercy of absentee landlords, and lived among laws that shifted with each political tremor from London or Dublin. Some years passed in uneasy peace; others were shot through with unrest that swept across Ulster like wind over dry grass.

"Ulster is a tinderbox, lad," John's father would say.

"You never know which spark will land."

It was not fear that drove them. It was erosion—the slow grinding away of hope. A man could work from dawn until dark, carve perfection from the hardest oak, hammer strength into iron, and still hold nothing secure.

This wore on young John Hamilton, the man who would one day become the immigrant patriarch.

He inherited the millwright's talent, the weaver's patience, and something else—an ache for possibility. He saw neighbors pulled under by rents that climbed each year, saw loom prices collapse under new industrial mills, saw men of skill and dignity reduced to tenants of their own crafts. And when news reached Armagh of ships leaving Liverpool for Baltimore and Philadelphia—of land cheap and broad, of work waiting for men who knew tools and timber—the thought struck him like flint.

He began to dream beyond the hedgerows.

It was around this time that he married Margaret Stevenson, the weaver's daughter with quick fingers and a steady gaze. Their marriage was simple, held in the local meetinghouse on a bitter morning when frost clung to the church windows and the minister's breath lifted in pale clouds. They left the service arm in arm, the Stevensons weeping softly behind them, the Hamiltons clasping hands in approval. The lane seemed changed that morning—wider, perhaps more forgiving—when they stepped into it as man and wife.

Margaret brought a weaver's discipline into their home. John brought a craftsman's fire. Together they built a household of warmth and labor, raising children beside a hearth that smelled of peat and flax, of oak dust and iron filings. Their cottage was modest, yet rich in the things that mattered: respect, partnership, and a determination not to let the old tensions of the land crush the young hope of their family.

But the winds of Ulster were not changing.

Work was thinning.

Land was slipping away.

And John felt the world tightening around him.

One evening, Margaret found him sitting outside with the moonlight falling over his hands, turning them silver and strange.

"You're thinking of America again," she said.

"Aye," he replied. "I am."

"What would we be there? Strangers?"

He touched her cheek gently.

"Or free."

It was the word that opened the door.

When the Hamiltons finally resolved to leave Armagh, it was not John alone who made the choice. Margaret stood beside him in the small room lit by the glow of the peat fire, her hands folded over the linen she had been preparing for winter. The silence between them was long, thoughtful—not strained, but weighted with the enormity of what lay ahead.

"America," she whispered, tasting the word like a prayer.

John nodded. "Aye. If we stay, nothing changes. If we go... maybe everything does."

Margaret looked around their cottage—the loom her father built for her as a wedding gift, the bundles of flax stacked neatly for winter spinning, the earthen floor she had swept clean that morning. This was the only world she had ever known. And yet, when she looked into her husband's face, she saw both fear and hope reflected there, and knew one thing with quiet certainty:

Where he went, she would go.

The days that followed were a slow unwinding of an old life. Margaret folded her linens with care, not as a woman leaving home, but as a woman carrying home with her. She tucked small comforts into her satchel—a carved wooden needle case, a bit of Armagh earth wrapped in cloth, a lock of her mother's hair tied with blue thread. John packed his tools and the small iron hammer that had belonged to his father.

The morning they left, the Stevensons and Hamiltons walked alongside them down the narrow lane. The frost clung to the hedgerows, the pale sun cracking between gray clouds. Margaret walked with her shawl pulled over her hair, her fingers clasped around her husband's arm.

"You'll write when you can?" Jacob Stevenson asked her.

Margaret embraced him tightly. "If the ocean doesn't swallow us first."

They laughed—quietly, soberly—but there was no mistaking the ache behind it. When they reached the fork where the lane met the old coach road, the families stopped. Jacob pressed the warm loaf into John's hands, just as before, and Margaret stepped into his embrace for the last time.

"Bring her back someday," he told John gently.

"If you can."

John hesitated. Margaret didn't.

"We go forward now," she said, voice steady. "No turning back."

Liverpool overwhelmed them both. The noise, the chaos, the brine-laden wind—they had never seen so many people in one place, never heard so many languages shouted across the docks. Margaret tightened her grip on John's hand as wagons rattled past and sailors cursed and gulls screamed overhead. She felt the ground tremble beneath her boots, as if the city itself pulsed to some unsettling rhythm.

"This is the world we're stepping into," John murmured.

Margaret lifted her chin. "Then we step together."

On the ship, they shared a narrow berth and a blanket that smelled faintly of salt. The crossing was brutal—gales shrieked through the rigging, waves slammed against the hull. Children cried. Passengers prayed. The air in the hold grew thick with damp wool, seasickness, and fear. But every night, when the ship groaned and tilted under the force of the waves, Margaret pressed her forehead to John's and whispered:

"We chose this life. We will see it through."

And he believed her.

When the storm clouds finally broke and sunlight pierced the gray Atlantic sky, John and Margaret climbed onto the deck, leaning against one another as the wind swept their hair back.

And then one morning, through a thin ribbon of fog, they saw land—green, rising, unmistakable.

Margaret caught her breath. "John," she whispered. "Is that—?"

"Aye," he said softly. "America."

Baltimore was louder, brighter, more alive than anything either had imagined. Wagons thundered over cobblestone streets. Women shouted from market stalls. The scent of pine and river water mingled with the unfamiliar tang of tobacco and city smoke. Everything vibrated with possibility.

John knelt, touching the earth.

Margaret knelt beside him.

He whispered, "Here I begin again."

She finished softly, "…and I with you."

Together they traveled north into Pennsylvania, stopping at farms and mills where their hands were needed. Margaret spun flax for wages or food; John repaired gears, shaped timber, and built water-wheels strong enough to withstand winter floods. They slept in taverns, lofts, barns—any shelter offered. And slowly, the land became less foreign.

In Chester County, they found hills that whispered faint reminders of home—rolling, green, alive with promise. The people welcomed them for their skill and honesty. Work came steadily. And in time, they built a life solid enough to stand on.

It was there that Margaret gave birth to their first American child.

They named him John Franklin Hamilton.

And it was from the hope, love, labor, and sacrifice of these two immigrants—the millwright and the weaver's daughter—that a story began.

A story that would one day lead their grandson toward the Maumee River, toward a town called Defiance, toward a destiny neither of them could have imagined the day they stepped onto that ship in Liverpool.

And now we turn to that grandson's journey—the man whose father never reached Defiance.

THE MAN WHO
NEVER REACHED DEFIANCE

Kirks Mills lay quiet in the early mist, the mill wheel turning with its slow wooden groan as the waters of Octoraro Creek pushed through the paddles. Even on calm mornings, the place seemed to hum—iron striking stone, gears clacking, saws singing, wagon wheels creaking over wet earth. Smoke drifted from chimneys in thin gray threads, and the sharp smell of cut timber hung over the village like a familiar cloak. It was a world of steam, sweat, and hard-used hands, a world built on the faith that industry—and not inheritance—made a man.

Among the boys who ran errands through that labyrinth of sound and grit was John Franklin Hamilton.

He had his father's face—that Irish sharpness at the cheekbones—and his mother's quiet steadiness. The elder John Hamilton, newly American after his Chester County declarations of 1817 and 1823, carried the old country in the cadence of his voice. In winter evenings, he'd sit near the fire with steam-burned fingers curled around a mug, telling stories to his wide-eyed son.

"Aye, Frankie. Liverpool was gray the morning I left it. Gray like a pot left too long in the rain. But Baltimore—Baltimore was gold. I knew the minute my foot hit plank I'd never go back."

He never did.

Young John listened as if he were hearing the ocean itself whisper across coals and shadows. But unlike his father—who had crossed seas in search of land—John Franklin was drawn to movement: piston rods, chimneys that belched steam, whistle cords that sang through metal, and rails that promised a straight line into a future still being hammered together.

He worked first at the mill, then with a machinist in Lancaster,

The Hamilton's of Ireland 🌿 97

learning the temperament of wheels and boilers. "He was never still," the old men said. "A lad made for engines, not plows."

And somewhere in those years—between the mill yard's noise and a gathering near Little Britain's church on a spring afternoon—he first saw Susannah Clarissa Iler.

She had the Pennock eyes—steady, watchful—and the quiet warmth of her mother, Jane Pennock Iler, who carried inside her the long shadow of Pennock, Levis, and Collett ancestry. The Iler girls were known for kindness, for dignity, for the way they seemed to still a room without ever raising their voices.

John saw her from across the yard, her shawl pulled close against a drifting April wind. She turned when someone spoke his name, and he felt something inside him settle—like a misaligned gear slipping suddenly into place.

"Are you the mill engineer's son?" she asked softly.

"Not his son anymore," he said, his voice gentle. "He passed two winters ago. But yes—John Hamilton."

"I'm Susannah."

He took her hand, and something quiet and permanent passed between them, as if two long wandering lines had finally found their meeting point.

A MARRIAGE BUILT ON HOPE

Their wedding was small—friends, neighbors, and a few relatives gathered in a clearing behind the meetinghouse. No grand ceremony. No wealthy benefactor. Just a simple exchange of vows beneath the old sycamore whose branches had watched generations come and go.

The Hamiltons had little. The Ilers had memories, heritage, and fields once tied to old Quaker names, but not much in the way of coin. Yet neither bride nor groom measured wealth that way.

They set up house near Kirks Mills in a modest one-room dwelling facing the creek. Each morning the smell of wet timber drifted through the window. John rose before dawn, wrapped his tools in a leather cloth, and stepped out into the sound of the mill wheel turning.

Life might have stayed quiet, ordinary—even content—if not for the rumor that began threading its way through Pennsylvania taverns and mill yards.

THE PROMISE OF DEFIANCE

By the early 1850s, talk spread of a line pushing westward—the St. Louis & Pacific, or one of its allied ventures—planning to cross the Maumee River in a frontier place called Defiance, Ohio.

"Rails clear to St. Louis," the men whispered over ale mugs.

"Good wages for men who know a boiler."

"They'll need engineers—real ones."

"Steam is the future out there, not water wheels."

For a man like John, it was not rumor. It was calling.

Susannah's younger sister, Nancy Henrietta Iler, was already in Defiance County, married to Aaron Blair, a millwright's son from southern Lancaster County. The Blairs had long been part of the Octoraro community—appearing in church rosters, land records, and harvest rosters. It was all too likely Nancy met Aaron at a mill gathering, a barn-raising, or during one of the shared harvest exchanges that tied Little Britain and Drumore families together.

When they moved west, they wrote home:

The soil is black as coal.
The Maumee bends like a silver ribbon.
Defiance is growing. Come if you can.
They say the railroad will need good men.

For John, the railroad promised the kind of work that shaped a life.

"Susannah," he said one night as they shelled corn beside the fire, "we could go. Your sister is there. Your mother may follow. There's more future in Ohio than there is left in these mills."

"And the danger?" she whispered. "Railroad engines are not gentle."

He brushed hair from her face, smiling softly. "Neither is this world. But out there, the danger has purpose."

She looked into his eyes—saw the same flame her Pennock ancestors must have carried when they left Ireland and England generations before—and nodded.

"Then we go."

INTO THE WEST IN AN OX CART

By autumn of 1851, little John Franklin Hamilton Jr. had been born (November 15, 1849), a bright-eyed toddler with his father's jaw and his mother's quiet will. And as the leaves browned and winter crept close, Susannah discovered she was carrying a second child—Emma—though the knowledge remained quietly tucked within her until the morning sickness made silence impossible.

They had no money for rail passage, no polished wagon. Only the loan of a pair of patient oxen from a neighbor and a rough cart that creaked beneath even modest weight.

What they owned could be tied down in blankets: John's tools, a few pans, one trunk, Susannah's Bible, scraps of baby clothing, and a small oil lamp that had belonged to her mother.

The world changed as they moved west.

Fields thinned into woods.

Woods thinned into plains.

Towns grew sparse.

Roads dissolved into rutted trails, sometimes no more than the memory of wagon wheels in drying mud.

They walked when the oxen tired.

They shivered in makeshift shelters when the snow came early.

They shared food with strangers heading west—German families, Ohio farm seekers, a handful of Irish workers who had fled the mines.

And each night, when they camped by a stream or beneath a stand of bare trees, John whispered the same word:

"*Defiance.*

Just think of it, Susannah—engines crossing the Maumee. Steel and steam and promise."

She smiled, rubbing her swollen belly, hoping he was right.

THE ILLNESS

Just past the Ohio line, the weather broke against them like a hammer.

Rain came first—cold, wind-driven, relentless. It seeped through seams, soaked bedding, chilled skin to the bone. John pushed them forward, insisting they make Mansfield before stopping.

"If we stop here, Susannah, we starve," he told her, though his lips were beginning to blue.

By the time they reached a tavern outside Mansfield—a timber-built inn with a leaking roof—John was burning with fever.

The village doctor, summoned from his small office, examined him and stepped back with the weary certainty of a man who had seen too many lungs give out in winter storms.

"It's a lung fever," he murmured. "I'll do what I can. Keep him warm. Don't let him lie flat."

For three days Susannah kept vigil.

She wiped his face with cool cloths.

Held his hand when the shivering came.

Whispered prayers her Quaker grandmother once taught her:

The Light is still with thee.

The Light goes not out.

On the fourth morning, as dawn slid faintly across the wet fields, John exhaled one last time—soft, almost content—and the room fell unbearably still.

WIDOW ON THE ROAD

They buried him behind the tavern, the ground softened by the rain. A simple wooden cross marked the place:

J. F. HAMILTON—PENNSYLVANIA

Susannah stood there long after the tavern keeper retreated indoors, one hand pressed to her unborn child, the other on little John Franklin Jr.'s small shoulder. The oxen waited quietly. The road stretched westward, muddy and silent.

She tightened her shawl, lifted her chin, and walked.

ARRIVAL IN DEFIANCE

When Susannah finally reached Defiance County, boots worn thin, cheeks hollow from cold, the Maumee River shimmered copper under a setting sun. The cry of a distant train whistle—thin and hopeful— echoed across the broad water. Men were already laying track for what they believed would be the great line to St. Louis, the artery that would pull goods and dreams across half a continent.

That whistle—the sound her husband had chased—rose into the air like a benediction.

Ahead, a farmhouse door opened. Nancy Henrietta Iler Blair stepped outside, hand raised against the fading light. When she recognized the shape of her sister, worn and trembling but still standing, she cried out and ran to her.

Behind her came Aaron Blair, shocked by Susannah's appearance, then quietly resolute as he helped her from the cart and carried the sleeping toddler inside.

A few months later, in that farmhouse, Emma Hamilton was born—John's child, born into the county he never reached alive.

THE HAMILTON LINE CONTINUES

Susannah would later marry Larkin Heacock, a union that would bind the Hamilton story to the Heacocks, and through Jane Pennock Iler back into the long chain of Pennock, Levis, Pyle, Sharples, and Penn.

But the Hamilton blood remained.

It lived in Emma.

It lived in John Franklin Jr.

It lives in all future Hamiltons

And it began with an Irishman who signed his petition in Chester

County, and a son who followed the promise of steam and steel across a winter-bound Ohio—a man who died on the road, but whose line continued westward, carried by a woman who refused to stop walking.

CHAPTER EIGHT

THE WIDOW
ON THE CANAL

THE LIFE OF JANE PENNOCK ILER

The boat rocked gently against the stone wall of the lock, water sloshing with a hollow echo that settled into Jane's bones like a memory. She sat near the stern, wrapped in a shawl that had traveled with her through sixty years and two counties, her small trunk at her feet, the initials *J.P.* still faintly visible on the lid though rubbed soft by time. Overhead, the towline creaked as the mules strained forward on the path, their hooves clopping rhythmically in the mud. A faint breeze drifted across the water, carrying with it the earthy scent of the canal banks, reeds trembling in the slow morning light.

She watched Ohio slide past her, lock by lock, bend by bend, heading always westward toward Defiance. She had boarded the packet boat alone, with no husband to lift the trunk for her and no children trailing after her skirts. To a passerby she might have seemed an ordinary widow seeking family in her last years. But inside her— beneath the shawl, beneath the gray hair pinned carefully in place— was a lifetime of silence, endurance, and memory.

The sound of water against the hull brought her back, not to Ohio, but to Chester County in 1806, to a moment she had never quite escaped.

She had been nine years old when the master of the poor school read her name aloud from the register.

"Jane Pennock." The head of household's last name identified the children of the poor school.

She still remembered how the ink glistened on the page as he dipped his quill, how the lines of children shuffled forward in the dim April light. The building had smelled of lye, boiled wool, and the faint, sour sweetness of children who had been crying. Beside her stood Isaac, only six, clutching her sleeve; Lydia, quiet and pale; Susanna—little Susanna—just five; and baby Ruthanna, restless in a caretaker's arms—all Pennocks by last name.

They had all arrived together on May 5, deposited like parcels from a family that had broken itself open.

She never fully understood the circumstances. No one explained why their father—William Pennock III, great grandson of Joseph the prosperous—had chosen another life over them. No one said what had become of their mother. The Pennock name, spoken with respect in other households, became for her a reminder that blood was no guarantee against abandonment.

The poor school demanded labor more than learning. She rose before sunrise to sweep floors that were never clean, washed linens that were always damp, and carried water from the pump until her shoulders ached. Nights were filled with the rustle of narrow beds and the soft sobs of children who dreamed of places they would never return to.

It was in those echoing corridors that she noticed a boy slightly younger than her—a thin, freckled child with watchful brown eyes. His name was Samuel Iler.

He spoke rarely, but when he did, it was in a soft voice that carried no spite. Jane remembered watching him help a smaller boy tie his shoes or silently slip his own portion of bread to a child who looked hungrier. Samuel had come from nothing—no heritage, no fine family name, not even the bitter pride of having lost something grand. He simply existed, a boy shaped by hardship before he had ever tasted hope.

Jane learned early that kindness in a place like that was a more durable wealth than land or lineage.

Years later, after they left the poor school, their paths crossed again—by chance or providence—on a stretch of road near a meetinghouse. He was taller then, with a young man's shoulders but a boy's earnestness. She was a woman working in service, her hands chapped from washing linens and scrubbing hearths.

Their reunion was awkward, hesitant, yet strangely familiar. His smile was the same as it had been when they were children—modest, patient, touched by something gentle. They spoke in fragments at first, until the conversation warmed like embers coaxed into flame.

Jane was older than Samuel by several years, but he looked at her not with the eyes of a boy remembering a caretaker, but as a man seeing someone who had endured the same bleak beginning he had. There was comfort in that recognition. More than comfort—there was possibility.

They married not in splendor but in necessity and affection, in the way two people who had once been discarded choose each other because neither understands abandonment as anything other than a wound to be healed through steadfastness.

They rented a small house in rural Chester County—a cabin of rough boards with a hearth that smoked in winter and a roof that thudded under spring rain. There, Jane learned the rhythms of ordinary life: the creak of the spinning wheel, the scent of boiling soap, the labor of hands that shaped survival from little more than will.

Into that life came two daughters, the only children she would ever bear:

> First Susannah Clarissa, born in 1824—bright-eyed, determined, with an inquisitive mind.
>
> Then Nancy Henrietta, born in 1832—steadier, softer-spoken, with her father's patience.

No one who saw the Iler household in those years would have guessed that both parents had once been poor-school children. Jane kept her past folded tightly inside her, the way she folded linens in the trunk she would one day carry to Ohio.

She watched Samuel age into a capable man, though hardship etched its trace upon him. He worked wherever work appeared—fields, mills, roads—never proud, always dependable. Yet seasons of toil and scant pay wore him down. By the late 1850s, his breath grew shallow in the evenings, and he felt cold even on warm days.

The fever that swept through the countryside that year seemed almost written for men like him—those whose bodies had little reserve left. It began with chills, worsened with a wrenching cough, and stole his strength hour by hour. Jane tended to him faithfully, pressing cool cloths to his brow, whispering words she had never dared voice before.

One night, when the hearth had burned low, he reached for her hand with surprising firmness.

"You'll go on, Janey," he rasped. "You always have."

She bit her lip because she knew it was true. She had survived the poor school; she would survive widowhood. But she would miss him. She had loved him in the quiet way people love when they have learned life offers little but each other.

When he died, the world changed shape around her.

She was no longer a wife, only a mother—and soon, a mother whose children had gone west.

The letters began arriving months after Samuel's burial

From Susannah first—stories of a young man named Hamilton, then the tragedy of his passing. Then news that she had remarried.

From Nancy—news of Defiance County, Ohio, of the confluence of rivers, of the canal boats that glided past mule bridges, of the new life she was building with Aaron Blair.

They both wrote with affection, but beneath their words, Jane sensed something more urgent: a desire for her to come.

It was Nancy's final letter, written in a steadier hand than her mother expected, that broke her hesitation:

> *"Mother, the winters are hard here, but we manage. I feel you should not be alone. Come before the cold returns. We will make room for you always."*

So Jane sold what little she owned, packed her trunk with care, and booked passage on a canal boat heading west. Rail was faster, but costly; the canal was slow, but certain. At her age, certainty mattered more than speed.

Now she sat with her shawl tight around her shoulders, watching the last locks fall behind her. The boat glided past farms, mills, and low bridges where boys called down to the passengers. At night she lay awake, listening to the mules grunting on the towpath, the slap of rope, the murmur of fellow travelers speaking in hushed tones.

She thought often of Samuel, and of the little girl she once was—the girl who had walked into the poor school with fear in her eyes and her siblings clinging to her sleeves. She wondered what that child would think if she could see her now—a widow traveling alone across the breadth of Ohio to meet her daughters, her past behind her like an old lock the boat had passed through long ago.

As the boat rounded the last bend and the landing at Defiance came into view, Jane rose slowly, gripping the railing for support. The mule bridge came into sight first, then the cluster of warehouses and mills, the canal water shining brown and steady beneath the late-day sun. A packet boat was unloading crates of grain; a group of children chased each other near the towpath. Somewhere nearby, a blacksmith's hammer rang.

Here, in this frontier town of rising streets and unfinished dreams, she was not the poor-school child, nor the abandoned daughter, nor the widow of a laborer.

Here, she was simply Mother.

CHAPTER NINE

THE QUIET JOURNEY OF JANE PENNOCK ILER

The canal boat slid into Defiance just as the sun began to redden the wooden walls of the warehouses along the towpath. The Miami & Erie lay still in the morning heat, a long ribbon of water that held the sky like a polished mirror. Jane Pennock Iler stood at the rail, her gloved hands tightening on the worn wood as she watched the shoreline draw near—strange, new, unfamiliar, and yet heavy with the promise of belonging.

She had not imagined she would cross her sixtieth year this way: a widow, alone, leaving behind all she had known in Chester County. But the world had changed around her—daughters grown, friends gone to the grave, Samuel taken by a fever that burned swiftly and left only silence in its wake. In the end there had been no reason to stay, and every reason to follow her heart west.

The boat bumped gently against the landing. A mule handler called out. Ropes were thrown. Travelers gathered their things. And then Jane saw them.

Susannah stood first, her shawl wrapped close, her eyes already wet. Behind her, Nancy Henrietta waved wildly despite her husband Aaron Blair's attempts to steady her enthusiasm. Two children pressed forward—one tall and serious, the other small and wide-eyed.

Jane's breath caught in her throat.

"John… Susannah's boy."

The last time she had seen him, he had been a squirming bundle barely learning to walk.

Now, at nearly ten, he was thin and earnest, with a gaze that reminded her painfully of the young man who had died on the road to Ohio.

Beside him stood little Emma, shy but curious, her curls catching the sunlight. Jane's heart trembled at the sight—her daughter's daughter, birthed in grief, raised in courage.

Larkin Heacock stood slightly behind them all, hat in hand, tall and composed in the manner of a man accustomed to both worry and leadership. Beside him stood Sherrod, his son from another life—a quiet boy of twenty with honest eyes and the broad hands of someone shaped by labor.

Jane lifted her hand. For a moment she could not move. Then the tears came, and she stepped toward her daughters.

Susannah reached her first. They held one another without speaking—grief, distance, and memory dissolving in the warmth of that embrace. Nancy soon engulfed them both, and Aaron chuckled softly, wiping at his own eyes.

"Mother," Susannah whispered. "Thee is home."

She spent her first nights at the Russell House, the inn that Larkin now operated on First Street. The building breathed with the noise of travelers—the scrape of boots on wooden floors, laughter from the dining room, the clatter of crockery in the kitchen, and the steady rhythm of footsteps on the stairs. Children's voices filled the gaps: Edward Byron's shouts of play, Ambia Dolly toddling after her mother, and the soft squeals of baby Alice, born only months before Jane's arrival.

Though the Heacock household welcomed her with warmth, Jane felt her age more acutely there. The Russell House was alive—gloriously so—but too full of motion for a woman who had spent decades in quiet cottages and modest rooms.

Yet those first days held moments she treasured.

One evening, as the sun filtered through the inn's tall windows, Susannah urged Larkin to tell his story to her mother. "She has never heard how thee came here," she said as she poured tea.

Larkin hesitated only a moment before he began.

He spoke of his birth in East Bethlehem Township, of Samuel and Esther Heacock and their devotion to the Friends' ways. He described the sweeping hills of Westland Meeting, where his parents sought connection across the frontier. Then the slow pull westward—to Short Creek Meeting in Jefferson County, where Quaker families clustered like beads on a string stretched across Pennsylvania's border into Ohio.

Jane listened closely, recognizing threads she had heard only in whispers—names, towns, migrations shaped by the same currents that had moved the Pennocks from Ireland to Chester County centuries before.

"And in Carroll County," Larkin continued, "thee knows of Mary Sherrod."

Susannah's hand tightened gently around her cup. Jane nodded, encouraging him.

He spoke of that first marriage—the early happiness, the quiet children, the creeping shadow of Mary's decline, and the heartbreak of her confinement in the asylum at Tuscarawas County. His voice softened as he described his decision to leave, seeking a place where he and Sherrod could begin again.

He spoke of his work in the Pennock businesses in Carroll County Ohio. This was where he learned his skills as a planer.

"Defiance was only a name on a map then," he said. "But mills needed hands, and the canal brought opportunity."

It had brought something else, too—Susannah Clarissa.

Jane looked at her daughter, who sat quietly beside her husband, her fingers brushing the rim of her teacup in soft circles. She had known sorrow early, but it had not diminished her—it had seasoned her like fire strengthens steel.

In the weeks that followed, Jane watched the rhythm of this blended family, the merging of past and future. Yet she felt herself an extra weight in the bustling Russell House. It was Nancy who finally said, "Mother, thee may be happier with us. The farm is quiet, and the children visit often."

And so Jane moved to the rural Farmer township, to the Blair home with its steady routines and gentle pace, close enough for Susannah's weekly visits and for John Franklin Jr.'s eager company. She also watched the growth of Aaron and Nancy Hentrietta's family and children.

It was from that place—quiet, green, and steady—that she witnessed sorrow once more.

Little Alice Heacock, the baby she had kissed upon arriving, died before her third year. The small grave was dug on a soft rise near the Auglaize River. Jane stood with Susannah as the wind curled the grass around their skirts, tender and relentless.

Years later, it happened again—Tecumseh Sherrod, only one, lost to whooping cough. Jane held his mother as she wept, her own heart breaking with memories of the siblings she had lost long ago.

By the winter of 1867, Jane's strength failed. An ulcerated stomach left her thin and weary, though her mind remained clear. Susannah visited daily; John Jr. came whenever his work allowed. He was nineteen now—tall, thoughtful, carrying the Hamilton steadiness in his posture and the Iler tenderness in his eyes.

She died softly, without pain, on a cold morning when frost clung to the edges of the Blair homestead.

The funeral was held according to Methodist practice—the Heacocks' chosen faith in Defiance. Jane was carried to Old Riverside Cemetery, to the Heacock plot overlooking the Auglaize River, the water moving slow and dark beneath the winter sky.

After the prayers ended and the others drifted back toward the road, Susannah remained. John Jr. stayed with her. They stood together, the winds sweeping gently up from the riverbank, rustling the dry grasses around the stones where Alice and Tecumseh lay, where Jane now rested among them.

Susannah touched the new headstone, her breath trembling.

"She bore much," she whispered.

John nodded. "And gave us more."

Mother and grandson stood in the lingering silence, framed by the soft murmur of the Auglaize, the wind carrying the beginning of fall's chill. In the quiet, the years between Chester County and Defiance collapsed into a single, tender truth:

Jane Pennock Iler had made her final journey home. Far from the wealth of the Pennock heritage.

CHAPTER TEN

REFLECTIONS OF
SUSANNAH CLARISSA

The porch boards were warm beneath her feet now, the last of the evening sun threading through the maples along East Street. Somewhere down near the Auglaize a train whistle drifted—thin, distant, familiar. Another sound of a world she had watched rise out of nothing more than mud, timber, water, and hope.

Susannah Clarissa drew her shawl a little closer, though the night was comfortable. It wasn't warmth she sought—it was memory.

She closed her eyes.

HER MOTHER, JANE

Her first thought, as so often in quiet moments, drifted to her mother. Jane Pennock, with her careful hands and her quiet voice, that strength tucked behind gentleness like steel wrapped in linen. A woman who had grown up with nothing—truly nothing—except the Pennock name and a fierce determination to hold her children upright in a world that had already abandoned them once.

Susannah could still picture her mother's hands on washday, red from lye soap, or the soft way Jane touched her forehead when fevers came. There had always been sadness behind her mother's eyes—the kind that comes from knowing your life began in shame not of your own making. And yet Jane never let bitterness settle. She worked, she prayed, she kept her daughters close. Even after Samuel died and the weight of widowhood returned, she still tried to smile for Susannah and Nancy.

And in her last years, when she came to Defiance and breathed the heavy timber-scented air of the old river town, Susannah thought she saw something in her mother soften. Jane died among family, among noise and grandchildren, not alone in Chester County's poorhouses.

It mattered.

It mattered deeply.

HER SISTER, NANCY

Susannah smiled faintly. Nancy Henrietta—spirited, stubborn, and loyal. Nancy could turn a small room into a lively gathering with only her voice and her hands working in the air. When they were girls, Nancy had been the one to chase off boys who mocked them for their father's reputation, to keep the little ones laughing even when dinner was thin.

Nancy had not changed. Even in Defiance she was still that steady flame—sharp tongue, quick wit, and a heart that wrapped Susannah's children in warmth as if they were her own. The Blair homestead in rural Defiance County had become a second home for Susannah in those early years, a place where grief could loosen its grip and where the bond of sisterhood felt like a quilt laid over old wounds.

Nancy was aging now, though she would never admit it. But she was still there. Still a presence. Still the one who had awaited her when her mother first stepped off that canal boat. Little did Susannah know that her sister Nancy would pass before the same would occur with her. Susannah would outlive her sister.

HER FIRST HUSBAND, JOHN FRANKLIN

Her breath caught a moment.

She did not speak of him often anymore—life with Larkin had grown large, full, demanding—but she never forgot the boyish grin of her first husband, nor the way he talked to machines as if they were old friends. John Franklin Hamilton had dreamed in iron and steam long before the railroad breathed life into Defiance.

She remembered his hands—blackened with oil, warm on her cheek—and the soft wonder in his eyes when he held young John Franklin Jr. for the first time. He had wanted a future that stretched wide, a place where his skill might mean more than a day's wage. Ohio had been his star.

And then the rain, the illness near Mansfield—the world narrowing down to labored breath and cold sweat. She had stood beside him until he slipped away, and afterward she carried their unborn daughter forward like a promise he had left her.

Even now, decades later, she sometimes felt him near when the train whistle blew.

HER SECOND HUSBAND, LARKIN—
BOTH PIONEERS OF DEFIANCE OHIO

Larkin Heacock entered her life like a mill gate opening—sudden, forceful, full of forward motion. He had been through loss himself; he did not hide it. And he had ambition, that particular fire of a man who had once worked wood and iron with his hands but now saw the possibilities of owning something larger.

He was never unkind to her. Never careless with her children. He had steadiness, and she had a mind for figures, for order, for the small decisions that made or broke a business.

He said once—only once—"Susannah, you're the reason our doors stay open."

He never repeated it, but she carried the truth of it quietly inside.

The Russell House, the Empire House, the Larkin House, and the Holgate House—all bore his name, but she had scrubbed their floors, planned their menus, calmed their guests, soothed angry travelers, and kept accounts that would make any banker nod with respect.

Holgate himself had praised Larkin for his reliability. But Susannah knew Holgate also noticed her—the competence, the respectability, the way she carried herself with a certain quiet dignity. Holgate would ask Larkin and Susannah to build the Holgate Hotel in the community named after him.

She had poured coffee for judges, shaken hands with railroad men, nodded politely to politicians passing through on packet boats. She had met canal captains swollen with whiskey, and she knew which travelers expected courtesy and which needed warning.

Her life had been far larger than the small house in Kirks Mills ever suggested it could be.

HER CHILDREN

Her heart always returned here—to the children who had shaped her days.

John Franklin Jr.—quiet, serious, wounded early by the loss of his father. She had watched him grow into a man with his grandfather's steadiness and his mother's sense of duty. He was careful with her, gentle even, and she felt pride each time she heard his measured footsteps on her porch.

Emma—dear Emma, warm-hearted and ever practical. The daughter who had given her a home in her last years, whose voice was the last she heard each night. Emma had endured losses too—the infant she buried, the hardships of a working man's wife—but she never complained. Susannah's heart tightened when she thought how soon Emma would stand alone without a mother to lean on.

Sherrod—Larkin's firstborn, forever caught between two worlds. She had tried so hard to be a mother to him, but his heart had always wandered. She prayed for him still.

Edward Byron—her eldest Heacock son, strong-willed, restless, always halfway down a road no one else yet saw. She had admired that in him, even when it frightened her.

Ambia Dollie Boody—her brilliant, complicated daughter, born in comfort in the Boody House in Toledo, raised amid the bustle of Defiance's hotels. There were shadows in Ambia, hurts she did not speak aloud, but Susannah loved her fiercely.

Alice—sweet little Alice, gone too young. Susannah still felt the weight of that tiny hand, the softness of that cheek. Some pains never dissolved.

Ulysses Grant—charming, spirited, a child who laughed easily. He had wandered west as a young man, chasing opportunity. She prayed the wanderlust had not swallowed him.

Tecumseh Sherrod—her smallest grief, barely a year old when he died. That loss felt closest to her even now.

Her children were her life's tapestry—bright threads, dark threads, frayed threads—and she loved them all.

HER FRIENDS

There were women whose faces drifted through her mind now— some alive, some gone:

Mariah Stevens from the miller's family where Larkin first lived and worked.

Mrs. Holgate, gracious and always curious

The canal wives, tired and sharp-tongued, who brought gossip with their buckets of river water

The Methodist ladies who had carried casseroles to her door when Alice died

They had comforted her when sorrow came. They had celebrated her joys. They had made Defiance feel like home.

THE TOWN ITSELF

And oh, how Defiance had grown.

She had watched:

> the canal become a vital vein for economic growth
>
> the mule bridge maintained for vibrancy of travel
>
> packet boats slide past her windows
>
> the courthouse rise on the square
>
> the opera house open in splendor
>
> the first gas lamps flicker into life
>
> the railroads come, screaming like iron dragons

She had watched William C. Holgate bend the town around industry and finance, watched her husband thrive under the shadow of progress, watched travelers pour into their hotels with pockets full of news from distant places.

She had lived a life grander than she ever expected.

AND NOW

She opened her eyes again.

Down the street a boy was calling to a dog, the sound echoing faintly between houses. The rails hummed somewhere north of the river, metal singing a low twilight note.

She touched the edge of her shawl, smoothed it once.

She had known hardship—yes.

She had known loss—more than most.

But she had also lived richly: in love, in work, in family, in the building of a town that had become more than a home.

And as she watched the shadows lengthen over Defiance, Susannah Clarissa felt something like peace touch her at last.

She had done her part.

She had carried her family forward.

She had lived a life that mattered.

And as the evening deepened around her, Susannah's mind drifted farther back—beyond her own marriages, beyond the children she had raised, beyond even Jane's weary courage—to the older stories that had shaped the very soil beneath her feet.

She thought of the Pennocks, her mother's people, and of the stories whispered in childhood about the old families in Pennsylvania. The Pennocks had walked near the Waynes—General Anthony Wayne's kin—long before Defiance existed, long before the Maumee and Auglaize rivers knew the sound of canal bells or rail whistles. It was strange, almost eerie, to think how close those families had lived: only a handful of miles between their farms, their mills, their meetinghouses. Lives running in parallel, never quite knowing how fate would bind them in a distant place.

Anthony Wayne himself—Mad Anthony, as the old tales called him—had stood on the very ground where Defiance now rose. He had built the fort that became this city, declaring defiantly that he stood at the "grand emporium of the West." His officers, his scouts, his soldiers had carved their presence into the land. And here Susannah sat now, an old woman wrapped in a shawl, watching trains pass the very ground where Wayne once stood.

How strange the weave of time was.

The Pennocks never knew that one day their descendants would settle in the town Wayne's victory created. They could not have imagined that their quiet Quaker blood would mix with the sturdy Heacocks, or that the children of those two Pennsylvania families would one day help build hotels, run businesses, guide travelers, and bury their loved ones in a cemetery not far from the fort built in the shadow of Wayne's triumph. As well the interaction of the Heacock's and Pennock ventures in the vibrant growth of Northeast Ohio communities.

And yet here she was—a Pennock by birth, a Hamilton and a Heacock by marriage, and a Defiance woman by choice and destiny.

Sometimes, in her still moments, she felt as though she were not merely remembering her life but remembering the lives that came before her—the footsteps of Pennocks in Chester County, the thunder of Wayne's soldiers along the rivers, the migrations westward that carried both families into Ohio's wilderness.

It humbled her.

It comforted her.

It made her feel part of something far larger than one woman's years.

The breeze shifted, carrying the faint scent of the nearby river, the same rivers that had borne soldiers, traders, canal boats—and her own mother, traveling toward a future neither could yet see.

Susannah let out a long, slow breath.

Yes.

There had been sorrow.

There had been struggle.

But there had also been legacy, the kind rooted in generations of endurance and unexpected convergence.

And as she gazed toward the place where the rivers met—where Wayne's fort once stood, where Defiance was born—she felt at peace knowing that her own life had flowed into that long, unbroken current.

THE RIVER
STILL REMEMBERS

The years turned, the century shifted, and the voices of those early pioneers softened into the hum of time. Yet Defiance—ever perched between the wide-shouldered Maumee and the quiet, enduring Auglaize—kept their stories in its soil as faithfully as any family Bible.

The old canal dried into memory, but its line still cut across town like a healed scar, reminding those who cared to look of the packet boats, the mule teams, and the bright lanterns drifting along its nighttime waters. The railroads came and thundered across the land, and later industry rose where forests had once stood shoulder to shoulder. But somewhere beneath every foundation, the imprint of the old paths remained.

It was here—on this patch of Northwest Ohio—that the long threads from Pennsylvania finally knotted into a single fabric. The Pennocks, once Quaker ironmasters and restless wanderers; the Ilers, born of little but endurance; the Hamiltons, steady and determined; the Heacocks, artisans and millers turned proprietors and civic leaders.

Lives that began in wholly different rooms of the American story ulti-mately stepped into the same corridor, drawn not by accident but by the quiet gravity of necessity, courage, and hope.

Susannah's children grew, married, scattered, and carried forward her unspoken lessons—industry, frugality, hospitality, and the con-viction that hardship was never a reason to shrink the heart. John Franklin Hamilton Jr. inherited her steadiness; Emma inherited her discernment; the Heacock children inherited her spark and her keen sense of capability. Each carried a piece of her handprint into the world long after her rocking chair stilled and her porch grew silent.

Defiance, too, bore the marks of those early years.

The hotels Larkin and Susannah nurtured, the properties they tended, the small fortunes they built and passed on—they all helped shape the rhythm of a town that once perched uncertainly on the edge of the Great Black Swamp. William Holgate's railroads, the mills along the river, the plank roads and early shops—all grew atop ground first broken by men like Wayne and held fast by families like the Heacocks.

And though most of the buildings have changed, though the mule bridge is gone and the opera houses are only photographs now, the rivers still flow as they did in Susannah's day.

The Auglaize still slides past the fort grounds of General Anthony Wayne.

The Maumee still widens into gold at sunset.

The wind still lifts the oaks and whispers through the grass above the graves at Riverside Cemetery.

There—beneath the shade of those ancient trees—Susannah rests in the Heacock plot, no longer far from her mother, the children she buried young, nor from Larkin, or from the family who came after. As well, the Heacock plot rests close to the William C. Holgate mausoleum, both founders and pioneers of Defiance, Ohio. And if one stands quietly at dusk, when the air cools and the river gathers its evening hush, it is easy to imagine the faintest echo of her chair on a porch, creaking gently, as though she were still watching over those she loved.

Because stories like hers never truly end.

They simply fold into the land.

They become the river, the wind, the quiet persistence of towns that survive.

They become heritage—unseen, but felt at every turning of the generations.

And long after the last canal boat slid into history, long after the railroads changed their names, long after the pioneers faded into photographs, the lineage she helped forge continues on—carrying her memory forward, one life, one telling, one descendant at a time. This includes James Hamilton, the author of this book.

HISTORICAL NOTES

B elow are clarifications regarding sources, uncertainties, and the historical framework used in constructing this narrative:

FAMILY ORIGINS & MIGRATION

- The Pennock family's presence in Chester County is well-documented; specific details about the early Iler family are limited. Scenes involving their early poverty and schooling are grounded in regional history rather than direct documentation.

- The timing of Susannah Clarissa (Iler) Hamilton's migration to Ohio is reconstructed from census data, obituary references, and family letters. Exact travel details are unknown; canal travel is historically plausible.

JOHN FRANKLIN HAMILTON SR.

- The cause and location of John Franklin Hamilton Sr.'s death are based on oral tradition and references within family writings. Records confirming the exact event have not survived.

LARKIN HEACOCK

- Larkin's early Quaker affiliations, first marriage, and work history are drawn from verified meeting house records, census data, and local histories. Some events in his emotional life and conversations are fictionalized for narrative continuity.

THE HEACOCK/HAMILTON CHILDREN

- Names, birth years, and death information for the children are sourced from census records, cemetery markers, and probate documents.

- Emotional reflections, motivations, and inner thoughts are narrative reconstructions.

DEFIANCE, OHIO

- Descriptions of the Miami & Erie Canal, the early industries, the opera houses, the mule bridge, and the development of Defiance County are based on historical sources.

- Interactions with prominent figures (e.g., Holgate, canal travelers, railroad men) reflect the family's documented proximity to these individuals but are partially fictionalized for storytelling.

ANTHONY WAYNE
& FOUNDING OF DEFIANCE

- The mention of Wayne and the Pennocks' proximity in Pennsylvania is historically consistent, though no record confirms personal interaction. Their narrative linkage is thematic, not genealogical.

PURPOSE OF THE NARRATIVE

This book preserves memory, culture, and heritage through a blend of fact and interpretation. Its intention is to honor—not certify—the experiences of those who carried these family lines across generations.

AUTHOR BIOGRAPHY

James D. Hamilton has devoted his career to strengthening the structures that support patient care. As a healthcare executive and consultant, he became a recognized leader in the development of physician-enterprise strategies—helping hospitals and medical groups align mission, finance, and clinical practice to better serve their communities. His work has guided organizations through mergers, growth initiatives, and cultural transformation, particularly in small and rural health systems where access and sustainability are most vital. He is the author of *Integrated Ambulatory Care: Key Growth Strategies for Small and Rural Hospitals*, and has written extensively on leadership, system design, and innovation in national industry publications.

Equally important to Hamilton is the preservation of history. His lifelong interest in genealogy has led him to document multiple lines of early American families, connecting personal heritage to larger national narratives. His research has supported membership and leadership roles in lineage-based historical societies, as well as contributions to heritage preservation and community remembrance projects. He believes that every generation holds a responsibility to safeguard its stories—to make sure that the sacrifices and values of those who came before us are not lost.

This book reflects Hamilton's enduring commitment to legacy. By preserving family histories, he seeks to honor those who shaped his world while offering future generations the gift of identity—an understanding of where they come from and what they carry forward.